"The papers won't be out yet. You've got a few hours to come up with something—something to tell your family."

"I don't need a few hours." The haughty face softened then, an almost apologetic smile brushing over his lips. "Because I already have a solution."

"Oh, no—absolutely no."

"You would want for nothing." He gave a devilish smile that had her insides doing somersaults. "Particularly in bed. Marry me, and I'll sign the resort back over to your father. Marry me, and your parents will have the peace they crave."

Mamma Mia!

Harlequin Presents®

ITALIAN HUSBANDS

They're tall, dark...and ready to marry!

If you love marriage-of-convenience stories that ignite into marriages of passion, then look no further. We've got the heroes you love to read about and the women who tame them.

Watch for more exciting tales of romance, Italian-style!

Available only from Harlequin Presents®!

Coming Soon!

The Italian's Suitable Wife
by Lucy Monroe
October #2425

His Convenient Wife
by Diana Hamilton
November #2431

Carol Marinelli

THE ITALIAN'S MARRIAGE BARGAIN

ITALIAN HUSBANDS

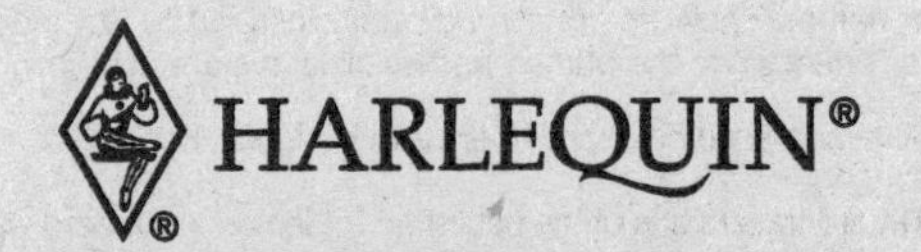

TORONTO • NEW YORK • LONDON
AMSTERDAM • PARIS • SYDNEY • HAMBURG
STOCKHOLM • ATHENS • TOKYO • MILAN • MADRID
PRAGUE • WARSAW • BUDAPEST • AUCKLAND

ISBN 0-373-12413-9

THE ITALIAN'S MARRIAGE BARGAIN

First North American Publication 2004.

This edition published by arrangement with Harlequin Books S.A.

www.eHarlequin.com

Printed in U.S.A.

CHAPTER ONE

HE WAS beautiful.

Opening her eyes, trying to orientate herself to her surroundings, Felicity knew there should have been a million and one questions buzzing in her mind. Her hazel cyes slowly worked the room, searching for a landmark, a clue as to what exactly she was doing in this elegantly furnished room, in this vast bed and—perhaps more pointedly, as one heavy arm draped more tightly around her—the question should be begged, what on earth was she doing lying in Luca Santanno's arms?

Santanno.

Just thinking that name sent an icy shiver down her spine, a fierce surge of hatred for a man she'd never even met, a man who with one stroke of his expensive pen had changed her family's lives for ever.

But for an indulgent moment before sanity prevailed, before questions demanded answers and the inevitable world rushed in, Felicity gazed across the pillow at her bedfellow, allowing herself a stolen moment of appreciation, a decadent glimpse of a man so exquisitely featured, so picture-perfect it was hard to believe that someone so beautiful could cause so much pain.

Beautiful.

From the jet hair that fanned his chiselled face, the long lashes on full, heavy-lidded eyes, to the wide, sensual mouth, a splash of colour amidst the dark shadow of early-morning growth that dusted his strong, angular jaw, every part of him was exquisite.

An involuntary sigh so small it was barely there escaped Felicity's lips as her eyes worked the length of him. He was tall. His olive-skinned feet, that should be encased in smart Italian shoes to match the dark suit trousers he wore, hung precariously close to the bottom of the bed, and his legs seemed to go on for ever. Felicity's gaze avoided the bit in the middle and moved straight to the white cotton shirt he was wearing.

The dark mascara smudge marring the crisp cotton spoke for itself—she'd been crying.

Worse than that, she'd been crying in Luca's arms.

The realisation truly appalled her. She never cried—never! Never lowered her guard like that. Raking her mind she tried to think of one exception, but none was forthcoming. Even when Joseph had died she'd kept a lid on her grief, refusing to go down that awful path, refusing to let out her pain. Her mind reeled in horror and she mentally fought to slam the window closed, to stop the images not only of last night but of the last few years from flying in, to return to the safe haven she had found, lying in the semi darkness with only beauty on her mind.

But images were starting to flood in—snapshots she didn't want to see, pictures she would rather forget—and the pleasant awakening she had relished for such a brief moment was starting to disperse as cruel reality broke through.

'Good morning.' Even before he spoke Felicity knew his voice—heavily accented, the slow measured cadence making those two simple words strangely erotic. Dragging her attention upwards, she found herself staring directly into the bluest eyes she had ever seen, and she felt the heat of a blush spreading from her chest, up over her neck to her cheeks. She wished she had used those hazy moments earlier to fashion a response to the inevitable questions that would follow.

'Good morning.' Not the wittiest of answers, Felicity realised, and nowhere near as sexy with her mild Australian accent, but it was all the fog where her brain had once been could come up with. He was pulling his arm free from under her, stretching out lazily on the bed, not even bothering to smother a yawn that showed a long pink tongue and very white teeth, as relaxed and at ease with himself as if he woke up with strange women in his bed each and every morning.

He probably did, Felicity thought as those blue eyes landed on her again. With looks like that and… She glanced around the room again, just in case her eyes had been playing tricks, but they hadn't; the heavy mahogany furnishings, the crystalware, the vast golden drapes all reeked of wealth and confirmed the fact that the man who lay beside her could have any woman he wanted—any woman at all.

And for a shameful, terrifying moment Felicity realised she didn't even know if she'd already been added to what was undoubtedly a long list.

'I expect you would like some coffee?' He didn't wait for her response, just picked up the telephone, reciting in Italian what seemed an inordinately complicated order for a simple coffee. Only then did it dawn on Felicity that they were actually in a hotel.

And not just any hotel, if she remembered rightly. She was staying at one of Luca Santanno's luxury hotels.

The question was though, which one?

'We are still in Australia, I assume?' she asked as

he hung up the telephone. 'This isn't the nightmare of the century and I've woken up in Italy?'

He laughed, actually laughed, and to Felicity's surprise she found herself actually smiling back at him, strangely pleased at the response to her vague attempt at humour. 'Yes, Felice, we are still in Australia. Your mystery tour stops here. I spoke in Italian then because Rico, who I was just talking to, is from my home town in Moserallo. There are a lot of Italians on my staff.'

'To remind you of home?'

He laughed again. 'No, my family has a lot of friends and a lot of…' She waited as he paused, and the words that came out made Felicity smile even more. '…a lot of wild cats and dogs backpacking around the world, who all decide to look up Luca for a job.'

At least she was in the right country, but the room she and Matthew had was small—not that it had seemed so at the time, but compared to this…

Matthew!

With a whimper of horror Felicity pulled the counterpane tighter around her, waves of panic threatening to drown her as she began to realise the true horror of her situation.

'I asked for some iced water also,' Luca said, apparently oblivious to her sudden distress. 'I expect you are thirsty.'

That was the understatement of the millennium. Her mouth felt as if someone had emptied a vacuum bag inside it, but even that was small fry compared to the heavy throbbing in her head the small movement had caused.

'Thank you.' Felicity sat up gingerly, pulling the heavy counterpane up and around her, acutely aware that all she was dressed in was some very small panties and a rather sheer bra. 'Thank you,' Felicity said again, clearing her throat with a small cough and wishing her mind would work, throw her some clue, some tiny snippet as to what on earth she was doing here.

'Are you all right?' He sounded concerned, his forehead furrowing as he looked at her closely. The colour drained away from her flushed round face as she sat up, blonde hair starting to escape from the French coil that had held it last night, petite hands moving up to her temples, which she massaged slowly, screwing her eyelids closed tightly.

'Actually, no,' Felicity said, taking a very deep breath and then exhaling out through her full lips, wishing the wretched room would stop moving for a moment so she could gather her thoughts. 'In fact I don't feel very well at all.'

'I'm sure you don't.' The concern had gone from his voice, the sliver of sympathy she could have sworn she'd heard retracted so sharply Felicity opened her eyes abruptly.

'Look, I'm so sorry—' Felicity started, her mind racing, words spilling out of her mouth. 'I really don't know what's happened. I'm staying here with…' she hesitated, unsure what title to give Matthew '…my boyfriend; we were at the award ceremony…'

He was staring at her, one quizzical eyebrow raised, as she struggled to make an excuse and work out how the hell she could get out of here with even a shred of dignity, how she could get back to her and Matthew's room and, more importantly, what possible excuse she could come up with to stop Matthew finding out where she had been…

'I think I must have food poisoning, or the flu or

something. I must have made a mistake and wandered into the wrong room...' Her voice trailed off as his other eyebrow joined its partner in his hairline, and somewhere at about that point Felicity admitted defeat.

'I've got a hangover, haven't I?' she mumbled, completely unable to meet his eyes, pleating the counterpane with her fingers.

'I would suggest so.' He gave a very small nod and she was positive, as his lip twitched slightly, that he was laughing at her, enjoying her utter humiliation. Felicity decided she had had enough. Coiling the counterpane tightly around her, ignoring the million hammers pounding in her head, she stood up. There was no point wasting her time with excuses. Whatever had happened, whatever awful mess she had got into last night, sitting here watching him enjoying her utter misery wasn't going to solve anything.

'I have to go.' How Felicity wished she was one of those sophisticated women she had seen in the movies. How she wished she could manage a mystical smile and sashay off as she blew a kiss. But waking up in a strange man's bedroom—in any man's bedroom, come to that—was uncharted territory for her, and her usually confident demeanour, the slight air of aloofness she generally portrayed, didn't seem to be surfacing this morning.

Tears were threatening now, but Felicity blinked them away. Whatever had possessed her to weep in Luca's arms last night certainly wasn't about to be repeated—and, sniffing none too graciously, she cast her eyes around the room in an attempt to find her clothes.

Skimming the room, she located her shoes and bag and hobbled over. The counterpane—wrapped way too tightly to merit a graceful manoeuvre but Felicity was past caring. She had to get back to Matthew, had to hope to that he was somehow as hungover as her and miraculously would not notice her creeping in at the crack of dawn.

'If you're looking for your dress, Housekeeping will bring it up shortly.'

It was all too much. With a small sob of frustration Felicity lowered herself onto the edge of the bed, resting her head in her hands. Her carefully pinned hair finally collapsed under the strain and unravelled in a blonde curtain around her shoulders tumbling across her face, and for a moment she took refuge under the golden curtain. For a second or two she welcomed its temporary veil as she tried to fathom how she, Felicity Conlon, meticulously organised, completely in control, could have made such an utter mess of things.

Last night had been planned down to the minutest detail. She had attacked it in the same careful way she tackled any job that needed to be done—determinedly pushing emotion aside, looking at every angle, checking and rechecking details until she was sure she had every possible scenario covered.

Last night had been business.

'I didn't just wander in here, did I?' Felicity mumbled, undignified memories not just trickling now, but gushing in with horrible precision. 'You carried me.'

'I did.'

'You were going to sleep on the sofa,' Felicity ventured. 'I didn't want to go downstairs—'

'To be with your *boyfriend*,' Luca broke in, his lips curling somewhat around the word. 'Right again. So I agreed you could stay here, in my bed, and said that I would sleep on the sofa.'

That much made sense. She'd got the four corners

of last night's jigsaw now, and was working on the bottom line, but the rest of it still lay in a higgledy piggledy pile in her cluttered mind.

'So why did I…?' He registered her nervous swallow, the dusting of pink on her far too pale cheeks and fought back a smile. 'Why did I wake up in your arms? Why weren't you on the sofa?'

'You asked me to share the bed.' Luca's voice was slow and measured, every word a scorching indignity as she screwed her eyes more tightly closed. 'I refused at first. Naturally I was concerned, given your…' a small cough, another sting of shame '…given your inebriated state and your lack of attire.'

'But you came over anyway.' Her attempt to discredit him, to exert some control over this hopeless situation, was quickly and skilfully rebuffed.

'You were insistent,' he countered. 'Most insistent.'

'Oh.'

'In fact you became quite hysterical. Rather than slapping you on the cheek, I lay down with you.'

'Oh.' He was speaking the truth. Ever if she'd doubted him for a moment, his words had set off a fresh cascade of memories. Luca begging her to be quiet; Luca pouring her water, standing like a protective parent and insisting she drank it; Luca pulling tissues out of a box, wiping away black mascara-laced tears… But through the murky depths of her despair a rather more disturbing image was taking shape. Luca taking her in his arms, holding her not gently, not tenderly, but firmly, clamping his arms around her, that beautiful methodical voice talking over her tears, on and on until…

Felicity took a shaky breath. She could almost feel the hand that had soothed her last night there on the back of her neck, working in small, ever-decreasing circles, massaging away the tension, the pain, working its way along her shoulders, soothing her as one might a child coming out of a nightmare.

But there had been nothing childlike about the response it had triggered, nothing innocent in the way her body had responded to the mastery of his touch. And, sitting there, dejected, embarrassed and utterly, utterly humiliated, Felicity knew there was one final question that really needed to be asked—one awful answer to complete her despair, one more nail to bang into the coffin before she made her way back to her own room and attempted to salvage something from the wreck that last night had turned out to be.

'Did we…?' Felicity swallowed, cleared her throat, looked him in the eye and squared her shoulders, ready to face the world—or, more importantly, her conscience. 'Did we do anything?'

'We talked,' Luca clipped. 'Or rather you talked and I listened.'

'I'm sorry if I bored you.' He didn't reciprocate her tight smile, made no attempt to elaborate further, and it was left to Felicity to pursue this most shameful line of conversation. 'So, if all we did was talk, how did I end up minus a dress?'

'When we first came back to the room I ordered some strong coffee. I was hoping it would sober you up. It might have worked had you not spilled it. Your dress is down with Housekeeping.' He put her out of her misery then, and if Felicity had looked up she'd have seen a surprisingly gentle smile soften his stern features. 'We didn't make love, if that's what is concerning you; though since you choose to bring up the subject…'

'I didn't,' Felicity argued, but of course Luca ignored her.

'Since you bring up the subject,' he repeated, his husky, deep voice halting her protests, 'had we made love, you most certainly wouldn't need to be reminded of the fact. When I make love to a woman I can assure you she has no trouble remembering the occasion!'

Shooting a glimpse from under her eyelashes, Felicity knew, as arrogant and presumptuous as his statement sounded, he was undoubtedly speaking the truth. There was nothing unforgettable about him—not a sliver of him could be labelled dispensable—and, however reluctantly, there and then Felicity had to admit that a night being made love to by a man as effortlessly sensual as Luca Santanno would be a night no woman could even pretend to forget.

'Thank you.'

'For what?'

Felicity swallowed hard. Still she couldn't bring herself to look at him. 'For not taking advantage.'

'Believe me, it wasn't difficult.'

Ouch!

'So we definitely didn't?' Felicity checked unnecessarily, her cheeks positively flaming now.

'We definitely didn't. I happen to prefer my women conscious.'

Felicity chose to ignore that particular little gem and, blinking a couple of times, felt what was suspiciously like relief start to flood her veins.

Things were still salvageable!

Okay, staying out all night wasn't going to go down particularly well with Matthew, and undoubtedly she'd have to omit to mention exactly whose bed she'd awoken in—after all, Luca was effectively Matthew's business partner—but the fact she hadn't slept with Luca offered at least a temporary reprieve. She would get her things and get the hell out, with hopefully no damage done.

Straightening her shoulders, she lifted her hair away from her eyes and flicked it back, forcing a tiny smile as she caught Luca still staring at her, even attempting to inject a flash of humour into this rather unusual situation.

'Whoops!'

He didn't smile back, just rolled over sideways, propping himself on his elbow, and resumed his blatant stare. 'Whoops?' he said in a very low, very sardonic drawl.

'I'm sorry,' Felicity ventured again, the watery voice now replaced by her more confident tones. 'You see, I don't normally drink—well, not spirits. The occasional glass of wine I enjoy…but as for spirits, well I don't even like the taste. I just had a couple for courage, you know.'

He shook his head and Felicity gave a small shrug. 'I'm sure someone like you doesn't need any help in the courage department.'

'I wasn't aware you had been drinking.' His words confused her, and she frowned as he continued, wondering if somewhere along the line she had misinterpreted him, if his English was really less fluent than it first appeared. 'Just how much did you have last night?'

'Two vodka and oranges.' Felicity pulled a face. 'And if this is what it does to me I'm glad that I don't normally drink. How could people do this for pleasure?' She was starting to ramble, the words spilling out from her mouth like a runaway train. She wished

Luca would smile, look away, shrug, even—anything rather than stare at her with that slightly quizzical superior look.

'You really think that two vodka and oranges could have that effect?' he asked finally, but when Felicity opened her mouth to speak Luca got there first, his eyes never leaving her face, watching every flicker of reaction as his words reached her. 'Do you still not realise that your drinks were being spiked?'

'You spiked my drinks?' Startled, she went to stand, but Luca let out a hiss of indignation, flicking one hand in a derisive Latin gesture and muttering something in Italian that Felicity assumed wasn't particularly complimentary, as realisation with the help of a few extremely hazy recollections, finally dawned. 'Matthew spiked them.'

The surge of anger that welled inside her didn't bode very well for the pounding drums in her head, and Felicity screwed her eyes closed as she grappled with this latest vile flaw in Matthew's personality.

Confirmation, if ever she needed it, of just how low Matthew would stoop to get what he wanted. The clanging gates of the prison door banged ever more loudly as she further realised the murky depths of his personality. Proof that the extreme lengths she was taking to curtail him were necessary.

Very necessary.

'My staff alerted me to what was going on,' Luca went on, but Felicity was only half listening—too busy concentrating on her awful predicament to concern herself with small details. 'You will remember I was actually sitting at the next table to you?'

'Mmm.' She gave a small shrug, a vague shake of her head, but as her blush came back for an encore

Felicity knew she wasn't fooling him. The earlier part of the evening was still fairly fresh in her mind, and six-foot-four of Latin good looks at the next table certainly hadn't gone unnoticed—even with a rather over-attentive Matthew at her side. The white-hot look that had passed between them when their eyes had met last night was scorched with aching clarity onto her mind, but she certainly wasn't about to inflate Luca's ego by admitting it.

'You ordered the non-alcoholic summer berry beverage that was on the menu; in fact you ordered three of them.'

'Yes, but like I said I had those wretched vodkas, and then there was wine with dinner...'

'Well, what you actually got was a questionable version of a strawberry daiquiri—and, more pointedly, three of them. Your partner made his way to the bar each time you ordered and told the bar staff you'd changed your mind. He also made very sure that he got a different member of staff each time, and it wasn't until he tried to change your order for the fourth time that one of the other staff overheard him.'

Felicity ran a hand through her hair, furious with Matthew, but more importantly furious with herself for not realising what was going on, for being so naive as to think that the illicit two drinks she'd partaken of earlier could have had such a huge effect. But her fury was starting to take a new direction now. It was all very well for Luca to take the high moral ground, all very well for him to dictate how his guests behaved, to dash in uninvited and play the proverbial knight in shining armour, but he didn't know the circumstances—Luca didn't realise just how significant last night had been for her and, more importantly, her father. She wished Luca had damned well stayed out of it and just let the night run its awful, inevitable course.

At least it would have been over and done with.

'I will be having a few stern words with Matthew this morning. If this is the type of behaviour he indulges in then perhaps he should look for other employment!'

A small groan escaped her lips. 'Please don't,' Felicity begged. It was essential Luca stayed out of it, imperative she persuaded him to leave well alone. 'He really didn't mean it. You know what Matthew can be like.'

'I have no idea what Matthew is like. How can I when I have met him two, maybe three times?' Luca shrugged dismissively but his features sharpened as he saw the question in Felicity's eyes. 'Has Matthew been saying any different?'

Oh, Matthew had been telling another story, all right. According to Matthew, he had a hotline to Luca—a hotline he was more than prepared to use if Felicity didn't toe the line. But that wasn't the issue here, Felicity realised. The issue here was damage control. She simply couldn't risk upsetting Matthew, couldn't risk her parents' stab at, if not eternal happiness, at least some semblance of peace.

Luca just had to believe her.

'Matthew and I—' Felicity started, her blush deepening with each awkward word. 'Well, we were going to…' Her eyes shot up, pleading for Luca to put a halt to this, to raise his hand and say that he didn't need details, that he'd got the message.

But Luca didn't. Instead he stood there haughtily, his lips firmly closed, looking right at her, her obvious discomfort at the subject not bothering him in the least.

Sinking her eyes to the ground, she settled for the less daunting sight of his feet as she mumbled what she hoped would be the conclusion to this embarrassing subject.

'We were going to get engaged…' Her voice was barely audible now, trailing off into a low whisper as she hopefully began to conclude this most difficult conversation. Casting a nervous glance up she saw the confusion in his eyes, listened as he took in a breath, opened his mouth to speak, then changed his mind midway and closed it again. 'That's why I needed a drink. I was nervous,' Felicity explained patiently.

But Luca, it would appear, was having trouble with his own jigsaw. Shaking his head, he opened his mouth again. Only this time the words that came out had none of his usual assured tones; instead he sounded utterly perplexed. 'Why would you be nervous? Why would you be so daunted by something so nice?'

'I just was.' Felicity shrugged. She certainly wasn't about to tell Luca the more personal details, tell him that Matthew had made his intentions very clear. There would be no more reluctant kisses on her doorstep, no more hiding behind her never ending excuses. Matthew was going to claim what he assumed was rightly his.

And there wasn't a single thing she could do about it.

Deciding she'd already said way too much, she stood up and attempted a haughty flick of her hair. 'Let's just leave it there, shall we? Could you please ring Housekeeping and have my dress sent up? I'd really like to get dressed.' She stood for what felt like a full minute, and when Luca made no attempt to reach for the telephone gave a shrug. 'Fine, it that's the way you want to play it then I'll do it myself.' Picking up the receiver, she ran a finger down the numbers before her, ignoring the holes being burnt into her bare shoulder as Luca blatantly stared. She didn't have to justify herself to him. If he wanted to go around playing the hero, he'd better just look for another damsel in distress.

'Okay, I can understand you might have been a little uptight,' Lucas conceded, resuming their discussion as if the most recent part of their conversation hadn't even taken place. Felicity hesitated momentarily, her hand poised over the number nine digit on the telephone. 'But why would Matthew want to get you drunk? What sort of a man would want to propose to a woman when she wouldn't even be able to remember it the next morning?'

She let out a low, hollow laugh, and Luca watched as her cream shoulders stiffened momentarily, her slender hand shaking slightly as it hovered over the telephone. He had to strain to catch the resigned and weary words, imaging those full lips pulled into a taut strained line. 'A determined one.'

The defeat in her voice, the utter exhaustion, stirred something within him. Suddenly his feelings towards Matthew, the so-called man who had annoyed him last night, shifted from distaste to disgust, from scorn to a black churning fury. But not a trace of it was betrayed in his voice. He realised that one misplaced word would have her back on the defensive, would have her marching out of his room and out of his life.

He didn't want her to go.

The realisation astounded him. Last night he had been concerned, as worried as he would have been at seeing any guest, any woman, being taken advantage of, being beguiled in such a way. But it was over now. He had done his moral duty, averted the problem. She was sober now, able to make her own calls. If she wanted her dress, wanted to go back to that snake's room, then why shouldn't she? What could it possibly matter to him what this woman did with her life?

But it did.

'You're not seriously considering going back to Matthew after what he did to you last night?'

'Look,' Felicity snapped, forcing a very standoffish smile as she turned briefly to face him. 'Thank you for your concern. As misguided as it was, I'm sure you meant well, but the truth is I knew what I was doing last night and I certainly didn't need your so-called help.'

'I beg to differ.'

Felicity's eyes widened, her eyebrows shooting up in surprise as his delicious Italian accent was replaced by a rather upper crust English accent.

'That is my London manager's favourite saying,' Luca responded, noting her surprise, but the momentary lapse in proceedings didn't last long. The onslaught continued in thick heavily accented tones that had Felicity scorching with shame right down to her toenails which she stared at in preference to the overbearing ogre that stood over her. 'The only sensible thing you did last night was to beg me for help. Me!' he shouted, cupping her chin with his fingers and forcing her eyes up to him. 'Perhaps you would like me to refresh your memory?'

'Perhaps not.' Felicity cringed, but her humour was entirely wasted on him.

'A colleague diverted Matthew's attention while I took you to one side and told you that your drinks were being spiked. You, Miss Conlon, promptly burst into tears and begged me to get rid of him, begged me for help, left me with no choice but to bring you up here.'

'You didn't have to do it, though!' Felicity interjected, brushing his hand away from her and facing him unaided now, but Luca hadn't finished yet.

'Believe me, I wish I hadn't bothered! Had there been a spare room in the hotel it would have been yours. Do you not think I had better things to do last night than play babysitter to you? Not only did I have a ballroom of guests to take care of, I had the press about to run a story— Damn!'

Without pausing for breath, without further explanation, he marched across the room, flinging open the door, and with her face paling Felicity realised she had pushed him too far, that he was going to throw her out—and what was more, Felicity acknowledged, she completely deserved it. Luca Santanno had behaved like a complete gentleman last night and she in turn had been an utter bitch. If she'd had a tail it would have been between her legs as she attempted to walk wrapped in the counterpane.

'Where are you going?' He didn't exactly haul her back in by the scruff of her neck, but it came pretty close. 'Where the hell do you think you are going?'

'Back to my room,' Felicity yelped. 'I thought you were asking me to leave.'

'I was getting the paper; I was attempting to show you why last night I had better things to do than play nursemaid.' Flicking through the paper, his face hardened, an expletive Felicity could only assume wasn't particularly nice flying from his lips as he hurled the offending paper across the room before redirecting his fury back to her. 'Is this the sort of man you deal with? Men who would throw you out into the corridor dressed in nothing but your underwear and a sheet? Is this how little you think of yourself?' Taking a couple of deep ragged breaths, he relaxed his clenched fists, the taut lines of his features softening, his words coming more softly now. 'Felice, this is surely no way to live?'

His fury she could almost handle—contempt too, come to that. After all, it was nothing she didn't feel about herself. But when his voice softened, the word Felice, almost an endearment, it brought her dangerously close to tears, dangerously close to breaking down. Her teeth were nearly breaking through her bottom lip in an attempt to hold it all in.

'I have to go,' she choked, utterly unable to meet his eyes. 'I'm going to ring Housekeeping to get my dress, borrow your bathroom for two minutes and then I'll be right out of here.'

Pushing the digit, she listened for the ring tone, ready to pounce when her call was answered and get her dress back so she could get the hell out of here, away from Luca and his endless questions. Her life was messy enough right now without this forced introspection.

But Luca hadn't finished yet. Hovering over her like some avenging angel, he held out his hand. 'Shouldn't an engagement be something special?' he asked as something that felt suspiciously like a tear slid down her cheek. 'Shouldn't the night a man proposes be a memory to treasure long into the future? Not some sordid affair, sullied with alcohol and regret?'

'You don't understand,' Felicity said through gritted teeth, wishing he would just stop, just leave her alone!

'I understand this much: if I had been about to propose to you then I would have been ensuring you were having a good time, treating you as a woman deserves to be treated, not sedating you with alcohol. Whatever the reason for last night, it cannot be a good one.'

His hand was on her shoulder now, but she didn't look at him. Reception had picked up, a voice somewhere in the distance was asking how she could help, but the only words she could really hear were Luca's. His words had reached her, and for a second so small it was barely there Felicity imagined herself in Luca's life, imagined being the lucky woman in his arms, imagined the bliss of being made love to by a man like that—those arms around her, that beautiful, expressive mouth exploring hers, his hands caressing her, that husky voice embalming her. The image of perfection only made last night seem even more sullied. The image of such wonder exacerbated the vileness of last night's potential union, and the truth she had chosen to ignore came to the fore as Luca spoke more eloquently than her own conscience.

'I understand you might not be…' He faltered for a second, trying to summon the right word, and Felicity sat rigid, her mind racing with indecision.

She knew she should get back, had to finish what she'd started, but there was something about Luca, something about the surprising gentleness in his voice, his insight, his abhorrence of Matthew's motives that held her there.

'…comfortable.' Now he had found the right word he spoke rapidly, determined to finish, to give her another option—anything rather than see her scuttling back to the excuse of a man downstairs. 'I can see that my presence is making you feel awkward, but that will soon be taken care off. I am due to catch a flight to Rome soon. I will ring Reception, tell them to collect your property and bring it here. They can tell this Matthew you have gone home—ill, perhaps, like you said before. This will give you some space, some time. Please Felice, I know I don't understand what has gone on, but surely you should think carefully before you go back to this man? Last night you were not just upset, you were distraught, and though I do not approve of Matthew's methods maybe he did you a favour.'

'How on earth did you work that one out?' She gave a low, cynical laugh, but it died on her lips as he carried on talking, as Luca once again summed up her innermost feelings in his own direct way.

'Last night you spoke the truth. Matthew's bed is not the place you want to be.'

And when he held out his hand again it only took a moment's hesitation before Felicity handed him the receiver, which he replaced in the cradle.

No matter the hell that followed, no matter the consequences, Luca was right.

Going back to Matthew simply wasn't an option.

CHAPTER TWO

A LOUD knocking at the door heralded breakfast, but, clearly used to staff, Luca carried on talking unfazed, while Felicity, in turn, sat huddled on the edge of the bed, scuffing the floor with her bare foot and burning with shame, appalled at what the waiter must surely be thinking and silently, fruitlessly wishing that Luca would put him right, tell him she wasn't yet another of his conquests, that his latest guest absolutely did not deserve to be the talk of the staffroom this morning, because, quite simply, nothing had happened.

Nothing had happened!

Of course Luca did no such thing. Instead he chattered away to Felicity as the table was laid, oblivious to her discomfort. 'Have something to eat,' he offered, but Felicity shook her head, determined not to accept anything from him. 'A coffee, at least? Or perhaps you would like a shower first?'

If he offered a shower again, if he really insisted, Felicity decided she'd accept; but when Luca merely cocked his head and awaited her reply she finally gave a small reluctant nod. Though it galled her to accept any crumbs from Luca Santanno, the chance of a shower was just too good to pass up.

He dismissed the waiter with a flick of his wrist.

True to form, Felicity thought bitterly; he was as dismissive as Matthew to his workers, but as the waiter left she blinked in surprise when Luca called out thanks in his thick accent, then turned the smile back to her.

'How about I make that call?' He gestured to the bathroom. 'There are robes and toiletries in there. Just help yourself and let me know if there is anything else you need.'

'I'll be fine.'

More than fine, Felicity thought, wandering into the bathroom, glimpsing the rows and rows of glass bottles that heralded a luxury suite—a rather far cry from her own toiletry bag, sitting forlornly in Matthew's room.

With a jolt she looked down at her watch, a mental alarm bell ringing to say that it was time to take her Pill. But with a flood of utter relief she knew at that moment her decision had been made; she didn't need to take the wretched thing, didn't need to worry about it any more.

Now she had finally acknowledged that she couldn't, *wouldn't* sleep with Matthew, the sense of relief was a revelation in itself—an affirmation of the strain she had been under, the turmoil behind the cool façade she'd so determinedly portrayed, the secret agony behind each and every smile.

Eyeing her reflection in the mirror—the wayward hair, the black panda eyes and swollen lids that just about summed up her life—she barely registered a soft knocking at the bathroom door.

'Felice, I'm sorry to disturb you.' Luca stood back as she pulled the door open an inch. 'I just need your surname. Reception want it for the computer.'

'Conlon.' She watched his eyebrows furrow slightly, his eyes narrowing as her surname registered.

'Conlon?' he repeated. 'Why do I know that name? It is familiar, yes?'

'Well, it is to me.' The thin smile didn't reach her eyes, and for the first time since their strange meeting

Luca Santanno didn't look quite the confident man she was rapidly becoming used to.

Snapping his fingers as he raked his mind, it finally registered. 'Richard Conlon?' Another snap of the fingers, another snippet of information. 'He owned the Peninsula Golf Resort.'

'Before you bought it for a pittance.' The acrimony in her voice made his frown deepen. 'I'm Richard Conlon's daughter,' Felicity explained, angry, rebuking eyes finally meeting his. 'I'm the one attempting to pick up the pieces after you destroyed him.'

Luca didn't need to snap his fingers now, details were coming in unaided. The underpriced resort he'd bought a year or so ago, the niggling guilt he'd chosen to ignore at kicking a man when he was down. Okay, Richard Conlon had brought it on himself, though he couldn't remember all the details his new manager Matthew had given him. Gambling, or drinking, or a combination of both? But whatever had caused his hellish debts, whatever had forced his ruin, it had never sat quite right with Luca, and now, as he looked into the face of his predecessor's daughter, the niggling guilt suddenly multiplied.

'It was a business deal,' Luca said, but his voice wasn't quite so assured.

'Sure,' Felicity snapped.

'I'm sorry for what happened, but it's hardly my fault. Your father was a poor businessman. He got himself—'

'My father,' Felicity flared, unbridled anger making her voice tremble as she met her enemy. 'My father was a wonderful businessman. He still is, come to that. The only reason the dump that the resort now is still survives is thanks to the hours my father puts in.'

'He still works there?' Luca answered his own question. 'That's right; I kept him on as a manager.'

'Assistant manager,' Felicity sneered. 'Second in charge to the wonderful Matthew. A man who runs the resort by fear. A man who pumps the profits into his own pockets instead of maintaining the place. A man living off the good will my father nurtured when he was the owner.'

'So why were you about to get engaged to him if he is so awful?' Luca demanded. 'Why did you walk in on his arm last night, half dressed and half drunk?'

His scorching words would under any other circumstances have hurt, would have lacerated her with shame, but in Felicity's present mood they barely touched the surface. Months of unvented fury finally came to the fore, her words so laced with venom she could barely get them out. 'Because your partner made it very clear that unless I slept with him, unless I came up with the goods, my father would be out of a job!'

'He is blackmailing you?'

'Yes.' Her word was sharp, definite—such a contrast to the question in his voice. 'Your partner is blackmailing me.'

'Partner? Matthew is not my partner.' An incredulous laugh was followed by a bewildered shake of his head, but it didn't last for long. Luca Santanno was obviously far more on the ball than Felicity had realized. His expression darkened, those blue eyes narrowing as he let out a long hiss. 'Is that what he has been saying?' When Felicity didn't answer immediately his voice became more demanding. 'Is that how this Matthew operates? How he exerts his authority? By letting the staff think he is the owner?'

'Co-owner,' Felicity corrected.

'Co-owner?' he blasted the word out of his mouth, like two pistol shots, and Felicity flinched with each one. 'He is not a co-owner. I am *the* owner! All the managers of my minor resorts have a five per cent holding; it is good for morale,' Luca explained his voice still angry. 'It ensures profit.'

'Ah, yes, profit.' Felicity found her voice, her hazel eyes flashing with distaste, meeting Luca's full on. 'There it is again! We're all very familiar with your love for that particular word.'

'Scusi?' For the first time Luca's English slipped, but he quickly corrected himself. 'What is that supposed to mean?'

'Profit,' Felicity sneered. There was no point holding back now, she was already in it up to her neck, but at least she could let this jumped-up, haughty, control freak know exactly what she thought of him and his methods—pay him back for the agony he had inflicted on her family. At least the final word in this whole sorry saga would be hers. 'That's the bottom line for you—and the top one, and the bit in the middle. Profit's why you pay your staff a pittance, why they have to stay behind night after night for no extra pay, why a beautiful resort is barely a shadow of what it used to be.'

'Barely a shadow?'

'Don't pretend you don't understand!' Felicity retorted. 'The resort is on its last legs—finished, kaput, *finito*. Now do you get it? Oh, I'm sure it's still returning a healthy *profit*. I'm sure on paper everything looks just fine. But the staff are leaving in droves and it's only a matter of time before the clients follow.'

The silence that followed was awful. Felicity reeled, scarcely able to believe she had admitted the truth, least of all to Luca, and Luca in turn paled, the muscles in his face contorting in fury, his knuckles white as he dug his nails into his palms.

'But what has all this to do with you? Why would you be ...?'

'Prepared to get engaged to him?' Felicity finished as Luca's voice trailed off. 'You dare to ask why I would prostitute myself with a man like Matthew?' She watched him flinch at her words and she enjoyed it—enjoyed watching the might that was Luca Santanno squirm. 'Because I'm my father's daughter. I see what needs to be done and I do it.' When he didn't respond she carried on, her small chin jutting defiantly, a stricken dignity in her strained voice. 'My father isn't the poor businessman you make out; he isn't a gambler or a drinker who frittered his money away. My brother was dying...' A tiny pause, a flicker of shadow darkening the gold of her eyes, the only indicator of the depth of her pain. 'The money my father made from selling the resort bought Joseph some time.'

'How much time?'

'Six months. There was a treatment in America—it was never going to be a cure, but selling the resort turned a few agonising weeks into six precious months. It took him to Paris and Rome, gave us time to say all the things that needed to be said, to cram a lifetime of love into six wondrous months, and if he had his time over my father would do it all again.'

'I still don't understand.'

'Death puts things into perspective, but it doesn't stop the bills coming in.' She was almost shouting again. 'Your mortgage doesn't disappear just because in the scheme of things it doesn't really matter. My father has had to start again, now has to work for a pittance for the Santanno chain, has to watch his beloved resort dissolve into nothing. But he doesn't complain. All my father wants is three more years of work. Three years to pay off his mortgage and get together some funds for his retirement—an honest day's work for an honest day's pay. But then what would the great Santanno empire know about that? All you care about is profit.'

'You are wrong.' Luca waved in abrupt dismissal. 'Yes, I care about profit, I am a businessman after all, but I also care about my staff, and in turn they reward me with absolute devotion. I do not need to check up on them, breathe down their necks while they work, for I know they are giving one hundred per cent.'

'They're giving one hundred percent,' Felicity snarled, 'because they're terrified of losing their jobs.'

'Rubbish.' If she'd seen him angry before then Luca was livid now, a muscle pounding in his cheek, his blue eyes blazing. 'My staff know I look after them. I ensure their birthdays are remembered, their loyalty is rewarded. Take Rico, the man I was speaking with this morning, it is his fortieth wedding anniversary next weekend. He will be staying in this very room with his wife, receiving the same service I demand for myself…'

'With a ten per cent staff discount,' Felicity bit back. 'Matthew reluctantly does the same.'

'There will be no discount,' Luca sneered. 'There will be no bill at all. Rico deserves it.'

For a moment she didn't respond, absorbing his words, his vehement denial confusing her. He certainly didn't sound like a man who mistreated his staff, didn't sound like the ogre she had envisaged. Her initial abhorrence was shifting. The layers of the onion peeled back were revealing a man far removed from the malicious man she had built up in her mind. But suspicion still abounded. The simple facts spoke for themselves—she had seen first-hand the devastation his leadership caused.

'This is Matthew's fault.' His voice was calmer now, but she could hear the hatred behind it, hear the venom behind each word. But his anger at Matthew brought only cold comfort; twelve months of pain were not eradicated that easily. 'I would never treat my staff like that.'

'But you have!' Livid eyes glared at him. 'Don't you understand, Luca, that you've done just that? Matthew may just be your partner—or manager, or co-owner, or whatever it is he calls himself—but it's your name on the headed paper, your signature on the cheques. You're the one destroying my father!'

'Sei pazza!' His expletive needed no translation. The hands that had been clenched grabbed at her wrists, pulling her towards him, but the fury she had unleashed didn't scare her, if anything it empowered her. She let her words sink in, gathered her shaking thoughts and took a deep cleansing breath before she continued, her voice calmer now, but still filled with unbridled hatred.

'Matthew has been blackmailing me.' She felt the hands around her wrists tighten, saw the fury burning in his eyes as she continued in low, steady tones, lacing each word with the contempt it deserved. 'He won't just sack my father; he'll destroy him in the process. He's made it very clear to me that he'll accuse my father of embezzlement if things don't go according to his sordid plans. He's already ruined my father's career, and now it would seem he's happy to trash my father's reputation if it will further his cause.'

'Which is?'

The hands weren't just tight around her wrists now, they were like two steel vices, and Felicity wriggled them free.

'Matthew considers it his divine right to have a pretty blonde wife on his arm.' She gave a wry smile. 'And if that sounds conceited I make no apology.'

'It is the truth,' he said simply, his mind temporarily leaving the devastating news she had just imparted and focusing instead on the attractive woman in front of him. 'You make it sound like a curse to be beautiful.'

'I never said I was beautiful,' Felicity corrected matter-of-factly. 'But, yes, looking like a fragile teenager can have its disadvantages, both on the professional and private front.' She stared at him boldly, her back rigid, her eyes defiant. 'Would you take me seriously in the boardroom, Mr Santanno?'

Her question clearly confused him, but he answered her promptly. 'I am not sexist. If your point was valid of course I would listen.'

He almost sounded as if he meant it, but Felicity tried and failed to bite back a scornful laugh.

'You contradict yourself, Felice.' Luca responded. 'You demand to be taken seriously, despite your stunning looks, while on the other hand you are prepared to get engaged to a man who wants you only for a trophy. It doesn't make sense.'

'I thought I could do it.' The scorn was gone from her voice. The directness of his observation was as loud as her own conscience. 'I really thought I could treat this arrangement as a business deal.'

'But in the end you couldn't go through with it.' It was a statement, not a question, but still she gave a tired nod.

'I'm not a romantic, Luca. I don't believe in the pot of gold at the end of the rainbow. I don't think there's a soul mate out there, waiting in the wings for me. Marrying Matthew wasn't saying goodbye to some long-held cherished dream; it was a means to an end, a solution to a problem.'

'For someone so young you have a very jaded view of marriage.' He shook his head in bemusement. 'What if he had wanted children? What if he—?'

'No!' She shook her head vehemently. 'I would never have given him a baby.'

'How can you be sure?' Luca demanded. 'How do you know he wouldn't have upped the stakes, demanded a child?'

'He could have demanded it till he was blue in the face, but that is the one thing I wouldn't have given him—whatever the cost to my father.'

'At least you thought that much through.' His eyes raked her face, searching for a clue in the chameleon pools of her eyes, for insight into this fickle personality.

'That's one thing that wasn't open to negotiation.' For an age her words hung in the air. Escaping his hungry eyes, she stared down, taking in the dark strong hands entwined around her slender wrists. She could almost hear the question in his unspoken words, the expectation in each rapid short breath as he waited for her to elaborate. 'I could never have had his child.' She turned to go, but still he held her.

'Tell me just one thing?' he asked, and as she reluctantly turned to face him he stared into those amber eyes, so wary and fierce. She reminded him of a stray kitten his mother had brought home, hissing and spitting, yet utterly adorable. 'How did you get to be so bitter, Felice?'

For a second she wavered, his harsh judgement searing through her. She wanted to scream at his injustice, to tell him he was wrong, but what possible purpose would that serve?

It was better that he thought her a hard-nosed madam, better just to walk away now.

'Years of practice. Now...' she gave a very thin, very strained smile '...if you'll let me have my wrist back, please, I'd like to have that shower.'

Oh, the bliss of the water as it slid over her body, washing away the caked on make up, the sticky lacquered hair. She allowed the tears she had held back so fiercely to slip unnoticed down her cheeks as she stood trembling under the jets, trying to fathom what she had done, the huge ramifications of the Pandora's box she had opened.

Wrapping herself in a soft white robe, she dragged a comb through her damp blonde hair. She was almost listless now, the unleashed emotions leaving her curiously drained. Staring in the mirror, she gazed at her reflection. The clear amber eyes stared back, for once unsure. The usually stiff upper lip was trembling as she attempted a mental plan of attack, a resolution to her problems.

She had really thought she could do it.

Really thought she could push emotion aside, ignore the awful implications of an empty engagement, do whatever it might take to buy her father some peace. But in the end she had failed him.

She pushed aside the internal ream of excuses that sprang to mind as forcibly as she pushed open the bathroom door.

There was no excuse.

Luca Santanno was right; it all came down to one simple truth: in the end she simply couldn't have gone through with it.

'I'm sorry.'

His words made her start, the sight of him pacing as she walked unannounced out of the bathroom unexpected.

'I am so very sorry for what has happened to you, to your family. I take full responsibility.'

He wasn't looking at her; the pacing had stopped now and he stood like a thundercloud, dark and brooding by the window.

'It's not your fault.' The admission surprised even Felicity. For a year now even the name Luca Santanno had caused her internal abhorrence, a fierce surge of hatred just on hearing it; yet now, standing before him, hearing his words, feeling his guilt, the tide suddenly turned and she knew her hatred had been misdirected.

'But it *is* my fault.' Dragging a deep breath in, he clenched his fists in a strange salute by his sides. 'You were right. It is my name on the notepaper; I am the one who writes the cheques.' His fists tightened more, if that were possible. 'And it is my name this Matthew has sullied. If the coffee is too cold, if the beds are not turned back, the pool too cool, it is *my* responsibility. Sure, I cannot be everywhere; I have to trust my senior staff. But when one of them…' He turned then, his eyes fixing on her; sincerity laced with anger, pride laced with shame 'For him to have treated you like this—' He thumped his chest, balled his fist against his heart. 'He is gone.' The clenched fist opened and he flicked the air dismissively. 'Gone. Dismiss him from your mind.'

'It's not quite that easy. Even if he's exaggerated, Matthew still has—'

'He is gone,' Luca said, with such precision, such a sense of finality Felicity almost believed him.

Almost.

Somewhere along the way she'd given up believing in people. Right here, right now, Luca was probably telling the truth, and Felicity didn't question it, didn't doubt that his apology was genuine, his outrage sincere, that he had every intention of following through. But in a few hours he would be back in Rome, back in his world, a world far removed from hers, and his intentions, however well meant at the time, would fade into insignificance.

She'd seen it all before—too many times.

Promises meant nothing.

'He's got a contract,' Felicity pointed out, her tone businesslike, addressing Luca as she would a client. 'There are unfair dismissal laws in place.'

'Would they have protected your father?' Luca responded quickly, quelling her argument with a stroke of his tongue. 'These are just minor details. My legal staff will take care of them.' He flicked his hand again. 'I promise you this, Felice...you will never have to see him again, never have to worry about that man forcing himself upon you, blackmailing you...'

'It's my father who is the concern here,' Felicity pointed out. 'I can take care of myself.'

'No, Felice, clearly you cannot.' He walked over to her, his eyes never leaving her face. 'Last night anything could have happened to you.'

'You're overreacting.' Her voice remained assured, but she felt rather than heard her conviction waver. Luca was right. Last night she had played a dangerous game, a stupid game, and her only saving grace had been the man who stood before her, the man who had rescued her. Her shift in feelings startled her, unnerved her, triggering a surge of adrenaline as she struggled with the impossibility of her emotions, praying for a voice of reason to descend.

She simply couldn't be attracted to Luca Santanno.

Surely it was a primitive response he had triggered? She was mistaking gratitude for lust. It took a supreme effort to keep her breathing even, to slow down her rapidly accelerating heart-rate as she urged sanity to prevail. It was gratitude she was feeling, nothing else, and it would serve her well to remember the fact. Clearing her throat, she forced conviction into her words. 'I knew what I was getting into.'

'Perhaps.' A muscle flickered in his cheek, but his voice remained soft—weary, even. 'What if it hadn't been my room you ended up in? What if another man…?' The muscle was flickering rapidly now, his mouth set in a grim line. 'What then?'

He searched her face, one hand moving up to her hair, stroking the soft blonde sheen, taking in the wide hazel eyes, so much softer without the sharp black kohl, the full rosebud mouth. The soft woman before him was such a contrast to the sophisticated beauty he had first laid eyes on, and it terrified him, truly terrified him what might have happened. The worst-case scenarios played over and over in his mind, kindling a surge of protectiveness, an immeasurable guilt for the pain he had caused.

'But nothing did happen.' Her voice was strangely high. She was trapped by his eyes, caught in the line of fire and, most surprisingly of all, with no desire to move. 'I ended up here with you.' A ghost of a smile trembled across her lips, but still she held his gaze. 'And you said yourself it wasn't difficult not to take advantage.'

'I lied.'

The simple admission hung in the air between them. He was moving closer now, his hand still on her hair, and the other one was working its way around her slender waist. She had every opportunity to move, every chance to step backwards, to brush away his hand, but instead she stood there, trapped by her own inquisitiveness, overawed and overwhelmed by the feelings he ignited. She could almost taste the thrill of sexual excitement in the air, the tingling awareness of her skin. Every tiny hair, every pore, every cell was saturated by his presence, thrilled and terrified at the same time as his deep voice washed over her.

'It took every ounce of restraint I could muster.'

It had. Closing his eyes for an instant, he remembered holding her, the bliss of her in his arms. He remembered comforting this delicious stranger, the protective feeling she had kindled, and later—when the crying had stopped, when she had curled herself up like a tiny kitten—feeling her hot breath on his hand, the swell of her breasts jutting against him, the tiny grumble as he had tried to move away, one infinitely smooth leg coiling over him, the scent of her, the feel of her. It had taken a super human effort just to lie there, not to respond to the subtle caress of her body. But now, seeing her without make-up, so young, so innocent, he felt the protective feelings that had smouldered, ignite now in a puff. The inevitable sexual awareness of a man and woman sharing a bed magnified. The groomed, sophisticated woman he had first encountered was gone, and in her place was a softer, gentler and infinitely more desirable version.

She could feel the heat of his palm radiating through her robe, pressing into the small of her back, and hazy, half-forgotten memories of the haven she had found last night emerged. The subliminal messages her body had unwittingly sent were more direct now. Her pink tongue bobbed out in a tiny flick to moisten her lips as her pupils dilated, partially eclipsing the golden rays of her amber stare, totality occurring seconds later as the force of his lips against hers obscured everything other than what was here and now.

He made her feel safe.

For the first time in so very long here was a man she could lean on, a man who maybe, just maybe, could make things better. Even if it was only transitory she welcomed the safe haven of his arms, the bliss of oblivion his touch generated. The chance to escape from the world for a while and concentrate on the responses he so easily triggered.

Responses Felicity hadn't known she was capable of.

As his cool tongue slipped between her softly parted lips, as their breath mingled, there was no question in her mind of holding back, no hope of restraint. She felt as if she were falling, freefalling, her body at the elements' mercy. But there was no fear, just a delicious feeling of abandonment, of freedom, of escape from the chains that had bound her for so long now. She kissed him back, her tongue moving with his, tasting him, and pressed her body against his as he scooped her up into his arms and carried her effortlessly across the room. She revelled in the strength of the arms that held her, the eyes that adored her.

At the bedside he paused momentarily, those sapphire eyes questioning, his voice thick with lust but laced with concern.

'You are sure?'

Reason almost stepped in then, sanity almost prevailing. She had never been intimate with a man, but her virginity wasn't borne of fear, nor some hidden desire to wait for the man of her dreams to come along. Relationships had taken a back seat to exams, to her brother's ill health, but now here she was, on the brink of discovery, and reason could go to hell. The need to feel him, to be adored by him, to be made love to by him, was overwhelming her. All she wanted was for Luca to lie her down on the bed they had shared, to make her feel every bit the woman she was, to instigate her into the pleasures of her body.

Oh, she was sure.

More sure than she had ever been in her life!

'Make love to me, Luca.'

The desire in her voice was all the confirmation Luca needed, and he laid her down, his breath coming in heavy gasps as her robe fell open, exposing her body. Her breasts spilled out from the soft white fabric and with a low murmur of approval he knelt over her, capturing one glorious swollen nipple in his lips, tracing the pink of the areola with his tongue as she tore at the buttons on his shirt, wrestled with the zipper of his trousers. She needed his skin against hers, to feel him, see him, all of him, and he registered her need, reluctantly leaving the soft sweetness of her breasts to free himself from the last remnants of his clothes. Turning his attention to her robe, he freed her from this final constraint so there were no barriers between them.

She held him in her hands, marvelling at the strength, and a tiny pocket of fear welled in her throat as he laid her back, slowly parting her legs. The weight of his body above hers was a precursor to the power of his erection. It would hurt, she knew it would hurt, yet she welcomed the pain, welcomed the sting of the first sharp thrust inside her, crying out as he moved deeper, wrapping her legs tightly around his waist, wanting more, more of him, for him to take her higher, deeper.

She could feel herself contract around him, a tight, intimate vice that held him, and the first ripples of her orgasm caught her unaware. The distant pulsing gained in momentum, a flush of heat surged up her breasts, stinging her cheeks, her neck, her ears, then rushed like a mass exodus to her groin. The flickering pulse was more insistent now, each throb a contraction that spasmed her body, feet arching, buttocks lifting. He slipped his hands underneath her, bucking into her, and she dragged him in, each contraction pulling him higher, further inside her, and as he let out a low, guttural groan her body instinctively knew how to respond, moving of its own accord now, drinking from him, sucking him dry, drawing every last precious drop from him, tightening around him as they rode the delicious waves together.

And after, as she lay in his arms, her hair spilling out across his chest, the tempest that had raged was calm. Her body was still tingling from its delicious awakening, and a sigh of contentment whispered from her lips as she revelled in a rare moment of peace and contentment.

Revelled in the solace she had found in his arms.

CHAPTER THREE

'WHAT are you smiling at?'

Closing her eyes for a decadent moment, she basked in the mastery of his touch, scarcely able to believe that one lazy hand gently brushing along the curve of her waist could render her so helpless. Lying beside him, it was easy to smile, easy to know that what had happened was good and right and perfect.

Such a relief to have no regrets.

'How do you know that I'm smiling?' she asked, her smile broadening as her words whispered along the soft ebony mat of his chest.

'I can feel it.'

He probably could, Felicity mused. She felt like an open book, lying in his arms, every page deliciously exposed. He seemed to know what she was thinking, feeling, needing, before she even knew it herself. Their lovemaking had been an utter revelation. Somehow he had known, instinctively *known* what her body unwittingly craved; every touch had been a masterpiece in itself, every delicious stroke an answer to an unvoiced prayer.

'So tell me,' Luca persisted, 'why are you smiling?'

'I can't believe that just an hour ago my one dread was that this had happened, that I might have slept with you, and just look at me now!'

'I am looking.' In one fluid motion he turned, gently flipping her onto her back, those expressive eyes making love to her all over again, scorching her as he dragged them the length of her body. 'No regrets?' he checked, his voice confident, only the tiniest movement of his Adam's apple indicating that her answer really mattered to him.

'Maybe later.' Felicity gave a small laugh. 'Maybe when I'm back at uni on Monday, or at my parents' for dinner tonight I'll have a major panic attack and scarcely be able to believe that I ended up in bed with you. But for the moment I'm just going to enjoy it.'

'You are a student?' She heard the gasp of surprise in his voice. 'Just how old are you?'

'I'm a mature student.' Felicity laughed at his discomfort. 'I know I might look young, but you don't have to worry about that. I'm actually an accountant.'

'Really?' A smile played on his lips and as he lowered his head just a touch, locating the hollow of her stomach with such precision, such skill Felicity found she was holding her breath, holding onto the bedhead for stability as he worked his way upwards. 'I thought accountants were supposed to be serious…'

'Boring, even,' Felicity said, the second word coming out on a gasp as his tongue found her nipples. 'It's a myth, but I'll admit to being serious. My career is important to me.'

'It sounds as if you take great pride in your work?'

'I do.' Felicity squeaked as his hand started to stroke the soft marshmallow of her thighs. 'That's why I'm studying at the moment.' She was trying to concentrate, trying somehow to explain to this wedge of hot flesh pressing against her that she was taking a year off to complete a Masters in Business Administration.

'Why would you bother?'

His question confused her, irritated her, even, and

she pushed his hand away, determined to answer him without distraction.

'Qualifications are important.'

Luca merely shrugged, his hand creeping on a steady march back, determined to finish what he had started, but Felicity was equally determined to have her say.

'Not everyone has the world handed to them on a silver plate, Luca. An MBA might seem irrelevant to you, but it's going to open up a whole new world for me.'

'Perhaps,' Luca conceded, dousing her indignation with one devilish smile, 'but the only world I want to open up is this one.'

His hand was more insistent now, pushing back her thighs he gently nibbled the pink swell of her nipple, flicking it masterfully with his tongue until the only Master Felicity wanted at that moment was one with a major in erogenous zones. But his arrogance still irked her, and this time when she pushed his hand away, when she struggled somewhat breathlessly to sit up, she meant business. The rather stunned look on his face didn't go unnoticed.

'You seem surprised?' Felicity quipped. 'No doubt you're not used to women halting proceedings during such a marvellous overture.'

'Felice…' A smile danced on the edge of his lips, and his body moved towards her to finish what he had started. But, seeing the determined set of her shoulders, the fire in those amber eyes, he thought better of it and instead raised his palms to the air in an insolent gesture of surrender.

'I'm sorry if what I was saying bored you.'

'It didn't,' Luca insisted. 'I can just think of better

things to be doing with our time than discussing your résumé.'

'But if I'd been a man no doubt you'd have paid more attention,' Felicity countered.

'Men don't offer the same distraction.'

'You're so sexist,' Felicity flared, but Luca merely laughed at her fury.

'Felice, you are lying in bed next to me naked; we have just made love. Now, if the fact I want to touch you, to taste you, to make love to you all over again renders me sexist, then I admit it—I am guilty as charged: Luca Santanno is a raging sexist.'

'Okay,' Felicity relented. 'Maybe my timing was a bit off; it's just that my work is important to me. Taking a year off to do my MBA wasn't an easy decision.'

'So why did you do it? Come on,' he insisted as she shot him a suspicious look. 'I really am interested.'

'Why?' she asked rudely. 'Why would you possibly care about my career?'

'I don't know.' The bemusement in his voice was genuine, and a frown crinkled his brow. Felicity found herself smiling as he carried on talking. 'I confess that diminutive talk is not a skill I nurture.'

It was Felicity frowning now—frowning and then smiling at his accent and choice of words.

'It's *small* talk, Luca,' she corrected. 'So, in other words, you generally roll over and pretend to be asleep?'

'Oh, I don't pretend.' Luca laughed. 'If eighteen-hour days have taught me anything, it is how to fall asleep at a second's notice.'

'But not this morning?' There was a slight hesitancy

in her voice, a questioning ring that both confused and excited her.

'Not this morning.' And this time when his hand reached and gently cupped her face she didn't push it away, just rested her cheek there, let him hold her in the palm of his hand as his deep voice washed over her. 'This morning I have no intention of sleeping, so tell me why you have taken a year off a job you clearly enjoy to study. Is your work sponsoring you?'

Felicity shook her head. 'Not financially. I've had to take out a loan to fund it.'

'That sounds expensive?'

'It is,' Felicity agreed, 'but it will be worth it in the long run. I could have done it part time, but this should fast track my career. Once I've finished my studies I'll be in line for a big promotion.'

'Which means more money?'

Felicity nodded. 'It would also have meant goodbye Matthew. You see, I never intended to stay married to him indefinitely. Just long enough to ensure I could take care of my parents—financially, at least.'

'Isn't it their job to take care of you?' Luca suggested gently, ignoring her sharp intake of breath and the fiery response in her eyes. 'Shouldn't it be the other way around? Did they know?' he asked softly. 'About Matthew, I mean? Did they know how much you hated him, the sacrifice you were prepared to make?'

'Of course not.' She shook her head fiercely, blindly, pushing the preposterous truth aside, but again Luca begged to differ. Cupping her face in his strong hands, he left her no choice but to look at him, no choice but to stare into those clear sapphire pools as he asked the question that for so long had haunted her, tapping into her Achilles' heel with such accuracy it had her reeling.

'They knew, Felice. Deep down they must have known.'

She bristled in his hands, bristled at such a cruel portrayal of her parents when there was more to them, so very much more to them. 'You don't understand—'

'No, I don't!' he responded arrogantly. 'I don't understand how they could have let this continue. The second I laid eyes on you last night I could tell that you were not happy. I could tell and I didn't even know you!' he rasped. 'Surely over the months they must have sensed your feelings? When I think of that lizard touching you, making love to you…' She could feel the hatred emanating from him, the anger behind each and every word, and she jumped in quickly, desperate to halt him, to redirect the fury away from the two people she loved most in the world.

'We never made love.' She saw the start of confusion in his eyes, and the hands that had been holding her dropped to his side as she continued. 'Last night would have been the first time—that's why I was so upset. So, you see, my parents really didn't know how much I loathed him.'

'But you were about to get engaged. He was going to propose. And you ask me to believe that you had never made love?'

'I'm not asking you to believe anything,' Felicity replied tartly. 'But it is the truth, Luca. That was how I kept him at arm's length. I told Matthew I wouldn't consider sleeping with a man unless I was engaged to him, and for a while it worked. I could cope with dating him—I didn't enjoy it, of course, but I just treated it as business.' She gave a tight smile. 'With absolutely no trace of pleasure.'

'But Matthew wanted more?' Luca checked slowly, and Felicity gave a resigned nod.

'He made it very clear that the dating game was over.'

'So last night wasn't just about getting engaged? It would have been the first time you'd slept with him…'

'Hence the two vodkas. I needed all the courage I could get!' Her vague attempt at humour passed without comment, and to her dismay she realised he looked far from convinced. He still believed her parents must somehow have known, have turned a blind eye to the appalling facts. 'Look, Luca, my parents really didn't have a clue what was going on. Matthew only made the threats to me, and it's not as if I've spent the past few months walking around in a state of nervous dread. Until last night I really thought I was in control, that I could deal with it, but when it came down to it I just couldn't go through with it. You were right to interfere. The truth is that I'm glad that you did. I may not be the world's most romantic person, but even I can see that losing…' Her voice trailed off as he stared, his eyes widening, a stunned, incredulous look paling the olive of his skin.

'Go on.' His voice was raw, and his hands were back now, but there was nothing similar to the gentle way he had cupped her face. His fingers bit into her, the tension in his body translating until he was practically shaking her, with an urgency in his eyes she had never seen.

'Luca, you're hurting me.' Her wail of protest, the tremble of fear in her voice reached him, and instantly he let her go, but his stance remained the same—blue eyes boring into her, every muscle in his body taut, his breath coming short and rapid, as if he had just finished a morning run. 'Are you telling me that last night wouldn't only have been your first time with Matthew, but your first time full stop? That you had never made love before? That you were a virgin?'

She almost laughed. A hysterical reaction, perhaps, but one that clearly wouldn't have gone down well with Luca in his volatile state. 'You make it sound as I've committed a crime!'

'You might not have, but I have!' Jumping off the bed, he swung around to face her and she reeled back, pulling the sheet around her, confusion drenching her as he gibbered on, fury making his accent more pronounced, tripping over the words in his haste to get them out. 'Where I come from it would be a crime for me to walk away from you now.'

'That's archaic,' Felicity shouted. 'This is the twenty-first century, Luca. You don't have to marry a woman just because you sleep with her. I would have thought you of all people would know that!'

'What is that supposed to mean?'

'Oh, come on, Luca. From the performance you put on this morning, even with my limited experience I'm quite sure that you haven't been saving yourself for marriage.'

'We're talking about you, Felice.'

'So it's different for men?' She gave a disbelieving laugh. 'I was right when I said you were a sexist. Don't worry, Luca, I don't expect you to follow up the morning's events with a proposal. My father's not going to ride up with a shotgun and shoot you at dawn.'

'Don't you see that this is something you should have shared? You should have told me,' he shouted, but his anger only riled her further.

'You make it sound as if I had some terrible disease,'

Felicity responded hotly. How dared he treat her like this? How dared he turn something so beautiful into something so sordid. 'You make it sound as if I've tricked you into you sleeping with me. For God's sake, Luca, you're overreacting!'

'No.' He shook his head firmly, proudly, even, as if she were the mad one! As if it was Felicity who had jumped off the bed in a furious rage for no apparent reason. 'I should have been told that you were…' His voice trailed off, as if he couldn't even bear to say the word, but Felicity had been quiet long enough, and she jumped out of the bed, facing his fury head-on.

'A virgin! You are allowed to say it, Luca.'

'Then why the hell didn't you? Why did you let me make love to you and not even think to tell me?' His lips sneered around each and every word as he practically spat them out. 'Did it not for one minute enter your head that I might want to know? When I lay you down on that bed, when I undressed you, kissed you, held you, did you not even think to tell me that this was your first time, that I was taking your, your…?' Angry fingers were clicking now, only abating when his word of choice finally made itself known. 'Your womanhood?'

Denial surged forth, but the truth beat her to it, and a nervous swallow drowned her lie as Felicity's solemn eyes met his. 'It did enter my head,' she admitted slowly.

'Then why didn't you say something?' he demanded 'Why didn't you tell me?'

'Because I didn't want you to stop.' The raw sincerity in her voice reached him, the painful honesty quelling some of his fury, and he stood there in defeated silence as she slowly continued. 'Luca, I wasn't tricking you. Yes, perhaps I should have told you that I'd never slept with anyone before, but the simple truth is that I didn't want you to stop, and maybe deep down I knew that if I told you you would have.'

For an age he stared at her, for an age he didn't answer, but when finally he spoke his words were gentler, the anger gone. The Luca she almost knew was back now—a touch sulkier, perhaps, definitely moodier, but infinitely more desirable.

'I wouldn't have stopped,' he said slowly, 'because I don't think I could have.' Sitting down on the edge of the bed, he ran a hand through his jet hair, then over his dark unshaven chin, and let out a long ravaged sigh.

'I wasn't trying to trap you,' Felicity said, tentatively joining him.

'I know,' Luca conceded.

'And I know I've got nothing to compare it with, but I'd say as far as first times go it was pretty amazing.'

'Even for a self-confessed unromantic?' Luca checked, a small smile softening his taut lips.

'Luca, I haven't been saving myself for marriage—well, not deliberately anyway. The line I spun Matthew was just that—a line. The truth is, between my studies and Joseph's ill health there really hasn't been much time for relationships. I can't believe I'm discussing this!' She swallowed hard as he turned to face her. Her anger had gone now, and all she felt was embarrassed and shy and utterly unable to look at him. Burying her scorching face in her hands, she kept them clamped there despite his efforts to prise them away. 'I'm so embarrassed.'

'But why?' he asked, perplexed. 'It is me who should be feeling shame.'

'I don't feel shame.' Behind her hands, she couldn't see him, and somehow away from his penetrating gaze it made things easier—easier to be honest, easier to say what she was really feeling. 'Embarrassment and shame are two different things, Luca. I'm embarrassed because…' Suddenly she felt like clicking her own fingers, attempting to summon a word, but instead she cringed as she forced herself to continue. 'I'm a twenty-six-year-old virgin.' She let out a wry laugh. 'Or at least until this morning I was.'

'And my overreaction to the news helped, I'm sure.'

A smile he couldn't see ghosted across her lips, and he saw her shoulders relax slightly, a tumble of blonde curls fall over her forehead, and chose that moment to gently prise her fingers away.

'Surely the very fact that you waited meant that you wanted to be sure, that you wanted it to be right…?'

'And it was.' Her eyes found his then, only this time she didn't jerk them away. What she had to say was too important to hide away from. 'Luca this morning was everything I could have dreamed of and more. Look at this—' she gestured at the room, the vast bed, the elegant surroundings, then her hand came back to his face, tracing his cheekbone with one long slender finger '—and look at you. You made me feel beautiful. You made me feel more like a woman than I've ever felt in my life. Our lovemaking was something I'm never going to forget and it's certainly not something I'm going to regret.'

An impish smile spread across her face. 'There is a down side to that, though. You've probably ruined my love-life for ever; I doubt anyone will ever match up to you, Luca. I'm probably destined to spend the next fifty years or so comparing everything to this one delicious morning and wondering why it doesn't measure up!'

He knew she was joking, knew she was just trying to lighten the mood, but his mind was working overtime. The knowledge that this gorgeous parcel of femininity, this warm, sweet body, was uncharted territory he alone had explored was almost more than he could comprehend. But hearing her speak of the future, imagining another man touching her, loving her, going where only he had been, fired something inside him, something black and churning. To a man who had everything it was so painfully unfamiliar it took a moment or two to register that the emotion assailing him now was jealousy.

'I cannot just walk away, Felice.'

'Then don't.' She was back in businesswoman mode now—back in control, back where she belonged. Pulling on the robe, she shot him a smile as she fastened the belt, flicking her hair from the collar till it tumbled in a golden curtain around her shoulders. 'If you really want to make this morning count all I ask is that you don't forget all about my father when you go back to Rome.'

'I will not let you down, Felice. I am a man of my word.'

'I hope so,' she said softly, heading for the phone again. 'This time I really am going, Luca—and if my dress isn't ready I'll go down and fetch it myself.'

'Why do you have to rush off?' Luca asked. 'Why can't you at least stay and have some breakfast?'

'Because, despite this morning's huge advances in becoming a woman of the world, I'm still a soft touch when it comes to goodbyes.' She flashed a smile but her eyes glittered with tears. 'No regrets, Luca. I really mean that.'

'So that's it?'

Felicity nodded. 'That's all it can be, Luca. You live in Rome, I live in Australia, and that's the smallest of the differences between us. Promising to keep in touch, to stay friends or whatever, would only cheapen things. We both know it isn't going to happen.'

'It could.' His voice was so assured, so positive, for a second or two she almost believed him.

'Let's not kid ourselves, Luca. Let's not make this any more difficult than it already is.' Her voice deliberately brightened. 'Who knows? Next year at the Santanno Hotel Awards it might be the Peninsula Golf Resort getting a plaque for ''Most Improved Hotel'' with my father on the stage receiving it.'

'Would you come?'

'I guess,' Felicity said thoughtfully. 'But then a year's a long time—who knows where we'll be then? I think some memories are best left, don't you? You get on with your fabulous life and I'll get on with mine. You might even read about me one day in the newspaper, when I make Accountant of the Year. One thing's for sure, though. I'll be reading the social pages with more than a passing interest now.'

She had said the wrong thing! The face that had been almost smiling suddenly darkened, and the mood plummeted around them; her almost dignified exit was disappearing at a rate of knots. 'What's wrong, Luca?'

'You just brought me back to the real world.' He gestured to the discarded pile of newspaper he had hurled across the room earlier. 'There will be a lot of fur flying this morning, and the trouble is I'm the pussycat.'

Felicity broke into peals of giggles. 'What's so funny?' he demanded.

'A pussycat isn't exactly how I'd describe you, Luca.'

'I hate this language.' His hands were back in the air now in a fiery Latin gesture. 'All these *stupidio* phrases you cannot elaborate on without making a fool of yourself. Where is the beauty in that?'

'You do very well, Luca.' Felicity attempted to soothe him but the laughter was still evident in her voice. 'So why's the fur flying this morning?'

'See for yourself.' Retrieving the newspaper, he handed it to her, then sat back down on the bed. After a moment's hesitation Felicity joined him, curiosity finally getting the better of her.

'Come on pussycat.' She giggled, peeling open the pages. 'One cup of coffee and then I'm out of here.'

Lying on his side, propping himself on his elbow, he watched her slowly turn the pages, smiling to himself at her little pink tongue, bobbing out as she forced herself to concentrate.

And it took one huge effort to concentrate! After all, arguably one of the world's most eligible bachelors lay a matter of inches away from her on the bed they had just shared, which made reading the paper just about the last thing Felicity wanted to be doing right now. Still, her interest was raised several hundred degrees as she hit the social pages.

The sight of Luca Santanno with a dark-haired, dark-eyed beauty on his arm shouldn't really have come as that much of a surprise, though. Since the day her father had come home, pale and shaking, and revealed the Santanno chain had made an offer on his property Luca's face had smiled at her from the newspapers, malicious and superior, the cat with the cream, but her hatred had gone now, and all Felicity felt as she stared was a curious surge of jealousy at the raven-headed beauty smiling seductively.

'I stand corrected.' Taking a nervous lick of her lips Felicity fought to keep her voice even. 'There I was, thinking you were only *arguably* one of the world's most eligible bachelors, but it says right here in black and white that you're in the top one hundred.'

'What else does it say?' His voice was gruff, and, shooting a look from under her eyelashes, she watched him wince as she spoke—even with the benefit of her hastily edited version.

'Oh, the usual sort of thing.' Felicity shrugged. 'A few choice words about your legendary playboy status, a couple of comments on your latest choice of date's impeccable fashion sense.'

'What else?' His words were like two pistol shots, the tension in the room rising as Felicity struggled to dilute the venom of the article.

'Not much.' She tried to keep her voice light, tried to sound impassive as she carried on talking. 'It just begs the question what were you doing in the arms of the newly married Anna Giordano while her husband is sick in Moserallo?'

'This is exactly what I was trying to prevent,' Luca hissed. 'My lawyers spent all of yesterday trying to prevent the paper running with this story.'

'Is this my fault?' Her voice caught in her throat. 'If you hadn't had to deal with me would you have been able to stop this?'

'That was my temper talking,' Luca said magnanimously. 'The first edition would have already hit the stands by then.'

She watched as he lay back on the bed, cupping his hands behind his head and giving an exaggerated sigh. Felicity wrestled her mind back to the article, trying to ignore the fact that even Luca's underarm hair managed to look sexy.

'The fact I blacked the photographer's eye after he took that picture probably didn't help my case. The best lawyers in the world can't stop the press when they've got the bit between their teeth—just ask the royal family.'

From anyone else his comment would have sounded conceited at worst, far-fetched at best, but there and then Felicity felt the gulf between them widen irretrievably.

Luca didn't just move in different circles; he inhabited a different world altogether.

Felicity deliberately didn't look up, not at all sure what he expected from her here. His hand had moved from behind his head now, and from the incessant drumming of his fingers on the bedside table Felicity knew he wasn't nearly as laid back as he appeared.

'Anna and I were lovers. In fact we were together for a couple of years. The papers didn't give a damn then, of course. She was Signorina Anna Ritonni then, so there really wasn't much for them to get excited about. Our mutual families were delighted, though, sure a wedding was just around the corner.' He watched for her reaction, but Felicity deliberately kept her face impassive.

'But there wasn't?'

'Not the one our families had in mind. Anna got married six months ago.'

'So it says here.' She made her voice light. The fact Luca Santanno hadn't held onto his virginity until

Felicity came along was hardly a shock—and what right did she have to make demands now over something that had taken place before they had even met? But even so her jealousy was curiously tinged with disappointment that a man like Luca, a man about whom she had only so very recently revised her opinion, would have run true to the form Felicity had previously predicted and committed adultery with his ex-lover.

'We didn't sleep together.' His voice was clear, his words measured, and the surge of relief that swept through her as she finally looked at him was inexplicable even to Felicity. 'And to avoid the confusion of earlier I will qualify that by adding "this time".' His dry humour didn't shift the tension an inch. 'Since Anna and Ricardo married I haven't slept with her—though not for the want of trying on Anna's part. The only problem is no one is going to believe me.'

'I believe you.' Felicity gave a small smile as Luca blinked in surprise. 'But why does this article matter to you so much? I hate to state the obvious, but you're in the papers every other week with some stunning woman on your arm; surely no one is going to bat an eyelid?'

'They will this time.' He let out a long, low sigh, one dark-skinned hand coming up and raking his short hair, then dragging over his unshaven chin before finally he spoke. 'As I said, we *were* lovers. Anna is my public relations manager—although—' he gave a tiny wry smile '—I think on these grounds I wouldn't have much problem dismissing her.'

'Careful.' Felicity wagged a playful finger across the bed. 'I think she might have a bit of a claim for sexual harassment there.'

He gave a low laugh, but then shook his head, and Felicity knew the time for joking was over. 'We are from the same village.'

'In Moserallo?'

Luca nodded. 'We both still base ourselves there. It's just a small village, but every time I go home I wonder how I ever left in the first place. It's nestled in the Italian Alps, and everywhere you look there's a view to die for, especially now, with the snow on the mountains.'

'It sounds wonderful.'

'It is.' Luca nodded. 'Of course the fact it's a three-hour drive to Rome means I don't get there often enough, and spend most of the week staying in one of my hotels. Though sometimes, if I'm feeling really homesick, I use a helicopter, which makes the journey almost manageable. No matter how luxurious the hotel, it can get too much. Sometimes it is nice to come home.'

'I can understand that.' Felicity shrugged. 'I can't imagine it, but I think I can understand it.'

He paused for a moment, those beautiful eyes narrowing as he looked at her thoughtfully, weighing up whether to go on or not. Felicity realised she was holding her breath, desperate to pass this imaginary test, to glean whatever she could about this difficult, complicated man.

'Anna was crazy about me,' Luca said, his words coming slowly, 'and I was crazy about her, but we didn't love each other. As much as she denies that, I know it to be true. Anna loved money, riches, the lifestyle. Not me.'

'Maybe she loved both,' Felicity said thoughtfully. 'The money and you?'

'No.' Luca shook his head firmly. 'A few months ago there were some financial problems—nothing huge, I had already foreseen them and taken care of things, but I didn't tell Anna that.'

'You were testing her?' Felicity, asked her eyes widening.

'Not at first.' He shook his head, but she could hear the hint of discomfort in his voice. 'I honestly didn't want to worry her, and as you have seen for yourself I don't really like discussing work when I am in bed. Still, she became more insistent, more…' Felicity waited, half smiling as again he snapped his fingers. 'More nervous. I realised she was worried I might lose my money, and even though it wasn't even a vague possibility I chose not to put her mind at rest, so, yes, I suppose in the end I was testing her.'

'I assume she failed.'

'She married Ricardo Giordano two weeks later. He is also from my town.' Luca's voice suddenly dropped and she saw his Adam's apple bob up and down a couple of times before he continued. 'Ricardo is also the closest thing I have to a father.'

Suddenly things seemed rather more sordid than complicated, and Felicity felt her mouth open slightly, her intention to remain impassive diminishing with every word.

'He is not in a relationship with my mother.' Luca grinned, realising in an instant the path her mind had taken. 'My own *papà* died when I was eight, and Ricardo has been the man I turn to for advice—I guess he is the father figure in my life. Apart from being a wonderful man, he is also exceptionally rich. He made his fortune in wine. Ricardo makes me look like a poor church mouse, which is why she married him.'

'You don't know that,' Felicity argued, though why she was defending Anna she had no idea—but given that she was tucked up in Luca's luxury suite maybe she could afford to be generous. 'Perhaps they just fell in love.'

'He is sixty years old.'

'Oh.'

'With a poor heart.'

'Oh.' Glancing down at the picture, Felicity shook her head. 'What a waste,' she said slowly. 'Poor Anna.'

'Hardly poor,' Luca pointed out, but Felicity shook her head more firmly.

'She is poor, Luca. Money can't buy happiness.'

'Anna thinks it can,' Luca argued. 'After all, it bought her a first-class ticket to Melbourne when her husband thought she was doing business at the Singapore hotel. She wanted to pick up where we left off, wanted us to still be lovers. I told her no, of course. I neither need nor want to sleep with another man's wife. The trouble is, this picture will be in the Italian papers now and any minute my mother will ring.'

'So tell her what you told me.'

Luca shook his head.

'It is not that simple.'

'Of course it is,' Felicity argued. 'If you really didn't sleep with her, your mother will know you are telling the truth.'

'My mother wouldn't mind if I was sleeping with her,' Luca responded, to Felicity's utter bemusement. 'My mother probably expects it! What will upset her is our lack of discretion.'

'Hold on a minute.' Felicity shook her head, sure she must have misheard. 'Your mother wouldn't mind you sleeping with a married woman?'

'Why would she? A lot of men have mistresses. It is our indiscretion she will not forgive. Shaming Ricardo so publicly—that is what is unforgivable. Even this so-called article—' he picked up the paper and tossed it across the room as Felicity sat there, blinking rapidly '—is better than the real truth. The fact that Anna cannot bear to be with Ricardo, does not want him near her and that still I rejected her, would bring the ultimate shame to all our families. Whatever way I look at it, it is a mess.'

'Goodness.' Nibbling the skin around her thumbnail, Felicity stared at the picture, scarcely able to believe that someone so beautiful could make such a mess of things. 'Is Anna worried?'

'She will be when she sees this,' Luca said darkly. 'I told her yesterday that she needs to respect her husband, her family. That it is definitely over between us.'

'And what did she say?'

'She agreed. She was embarrassed, a bit upset. And when I spoke to her, told her how I felt, she begged me not to let anyone find out. I think she finally realised she must work at her marriage.'

Felicity doubted that. Being rejected by Luca would hurt like hell. She had only spent one night in his arms and already she was out of her depth. To have known such perfection for two years and then have it snatched away—well, it defied rational thought.

Picking up the paper, Felicity stared at the picture once more. Anna's dark calculating eyes sent a shiver of mistrust through her.

Anna had more than saving her marriage on her mind.

'I tell you, when my mother reads this she will go crazy.' Luca's worried voice broke into her thoughts and Felicity smothered a smile. But it was too late for Luca's sharp eyes. 'What is so funny?' he demanded.

'You just don't seem like the sort of man who'd be worried about what his mother would think.'

'Why? Do you think a man can only be macho if he disregards the people he loves?' Luca snapped as Felicity swallowed her response. 'That I should not care if I shame my mother, if I disappoint her? These press don't know the hell they create. You are not the only one who cares about their parents, Felice. My mother is older now, she wants her son married, settled, yet she turns a blind eye, accepts I am not ready to settle down. But when she thinks I am sleeping with a family friend's wife and not even bothering to be discreet, then…' He stood up, and this time he did pull on a robe, tying the belt in fury. The incessant pacing started again as Felicity looked on. 'Then I hurt her.'

'It's night time in Italy.' Her small voice stopped him in his tracks. Swinging around, he shot her an incredulous look.

'What the hell has that got to do with it?'

'The papers won't be out yet. You've got a few hours to come up with something—something to tell your family.'

'I don't need a few hours.' The haughty face softened then, an almost apologetic smile brushing over lips. 'Because I already have a solution.'

'You do?' Smiling, Felicity sat straighter, perking up with interest. 'Well, why didn't you say so?'

He didn't answer, just walked over and sat down, one hand pulling hers across the bed, those dark blue eyes staring intently now. The bob of his Adam's apple as he cleared his throat made Felicity suddenly awash with the strangest sense of foreboding, the weirdest feeling that his solution wasn't a simple one.

'Anna and I could be just friends,' he started, and Felicity's eyes darted nervously. 'Perhaps if I had fallen head over heels in love, it wouldn't be out of the question for her to have flown over for a bit of feminine insight.'

'Insight?' Felicity squeaked, her mind working overtime, his calculated words coming too fast at her.

'Insight,' Luca repeated. 'I'm hopeless with jewellery, things like that, and with something as important as an engagement ring I'd want to get it right.'

Alarm bells weren't just ringing now, they were clanging. Her eyes widened as she shrank back on the bed, shaking her head wildly as Luca sweetened his words with the softest of smiles. 'Oh, no. Absolutely no.'

'But it would solve everything,' Luca said, his voice completely calm, as if he had suggested they pop out to the shops or perhaps call down for some cake. 'And in the meantime we could have some fun.'

'And exactly how long is this "fun" supposed to last?' Before the inevitable shrug had even left his shoulders Felicity broke in. 'It's a reasonable question, Luca.'

'You could do your studies by correspondence, see the world with me. We get on so well together.'

'We've only been together one night, and for most of that we were asleep!'

'At least you can read the newspaper in silence. Have you any idea what an impossible feat that is for some women?' A poor imitation of a female voice followed. '"Luca, wasn't last night special? Luca, what shall we do today? Luca, what would you like for dinner?"'

A tiny laugh softened her strained features. 'That's called insecurity, Luca; they were probably trying to make sure there would be another night, that you were actually coming back.'

'I probably would have, if they'd just let me read in peace.'

'And I suppose that would be one of the rules?' Her voice was sharp, to the point, and Luca frowned as Felicity carried on talking. 'That I'd have to eat my breakfast in silence? That I mustn't ask about the master's plans for the day—'

'You are twisting my words,' Luca broke in. 'You are making me out as some sort of monster. I would treat you wonderfully—better than that *bastardo* Matthew. You would want for nothing.' He gave a devilish smile that had her insides doing somersaults. 'Particularly in bed.'

'I'd be a glorified mistress,' Felicity responded, distaste curling her lips, but Luca merely smiled.

'A mistress with a ring, though. Have you any idea the power that would wield? Have you any idea the doors that would open for you?'

'I don't want doors to open for me, I'm happy turning the handles myself, Luca.' She knew she had confused him, but Felicity was past caring, her mind focused instead on telling this spoilt playboy in no uncertain terms that for once in his life the answer was most definitely no! 'I don't mind working for a living. I don't mind staying up all night studying if I have to. I happen to like my life.'

'It didn't look that way last night.' Luca's voice stilled her outburst. 'In fact last night you'd have given just about anything to change it. And now you can,' he said simply. 'Marry me and I'll sign the resort back over to your father. Marry me and your parents will have the peace they crave.'

He paused, and for the first time Felicity didn't jump in to fill it. Instead she sat in stunned silence, scarcely able to fathom she was even considering this outrageous request, scarcely able to believe she was seriously contemplating it.

'Marry me,' he said softly.

'Is this because we slept together?' Felicity asked. 'Is this some misguided sense of honour…?'

'There is nothing misguided about honour,' Luca said smartly. 'I took your womanhood; it is right that I marry you.'

'It's archaic,' Felicity retorted, 'and it is also completely unnecessary.'

'Just think about it for a moment.' His voice was still soft, but there was a power she couldn't identify behind it, a note of absolute determination that told Felicity that the power Luca yielded wasn't just confined to the boardroom. For despite her initial abhorrence, despite the abundance of questions flooding her usually ordered mind, a flutter of excitement welled in the pit of her stomach. The prospect of lying next to Luca each night, seeing the world through his sophisticated eyes, holding him, adoring him, being made love to by him again and again…

'I'm not asking for forever here—just long enough to put things right, for both of us,' he added softly. 'You will save not only my family, but Ricardo too from being shamed. Now, that doesn't mean a thing to you and I understand that completely, but I would be indebted to you—I will make your father owner of the resort again; I'll get my lawyers on to it first thing on Monday. And as for honour…' He drew a deep, ragged breath, his eyes holding hers with a sincerity that reached for her soul. 'Call it archaic, call it what you will, but I cannot just walk away now…'

'But you will walk away one day, Luca,' Felicity pointed out, ignoring the icy fingers of fear that wrapped around her heart at the prospect. 'What does that do to your argument? Where's the honour in being divorced?'

'You will have slept only with one man,' Luca responded swiftly. 'And that man will have been your husband. I would say there's plenty of honour in that.'

He held her at arm's length then, his eyes searing her with their clarity. 'You would come into this marriage with no hidden threats, no secret agenda…' He was like a runaway train, gaining momentum with each and every forward motion. The germ of an idea that had emerged was taking shape, crystal-clear shape, and seeing her sitting on his bed, so cute, so utterly, utterly adorable, all Luca knew was that he couldn't let her go, couldn't let this blonde beauty walk out of the room and out of his life.

Nothing else mattered. Nothing else made any sense.

'There will be no false declarations of love, no babies clouding the issue, no promises of for ever—just a mutual respect and understanding. Felice, I will be strong for you. I *will* make this work.'

Suspicious eyes turned up to him then, but his strength, his quiet dignity were more of an aphrodisiac than the love he had so skilfully made.

Sensing weakness, he let a teasing smile creep over his face, and his low, sexy voice almost masked the humour behind his words. 'And I don't doubt for a second that I am far better in bed than Matthew would ever have been.'

Of all the pompous— The words were on the tip of her tongue, but so was Luca, his lips forcing hers apart, the hand that had been holding hers dragging her forward, into his arms and into his life—and every eloquent argument that had formed in her mind was reduced to a quivering mass of jelly as she landed on his lap.

Her gown fell open as his hands greedily claimed the rising swell of her breasts, the velvet steel of his erection parting the robe, nudging its way in uninvited but terribly, shamefully welcome. Her head flailed backwards as his lips moved down, blazing a trail over her neck, and his fingers worked their magic further down, causing her to cry out in reluctant ecstasy as he located the flickering swollen nub of her womanhood.

'Is that a yes?'

The genius of his lovemaking, the mastery of his touch awoke so much more than passion in her. Here was a man who made the terribly complicated straightforward all of sudden, propelled her into a stratosphere where rules didn't matter, where surely all could be conquered. She had always been passionate about Luca, however misdirected, and though the hate she had felt had shifted now, the passion remained; only this time it looked something suspiciously like love.

'Is that a yes?' he demanded again, his voice hoarse, his manhood swollen at her entrance, awaiting her answer.

She felt as if she were falling again, freefalling into dangerous, forbidden but decadently tempting territory, and she waited for her mental safety chute to open, for sanity to prevail, for her usually meticulous and ordered mind to register its protest, to tell her she was falling out of the frying pan into the fire.

Oh, but what a fire.

Luca was the man who could put things to right, the man who had saved her from herself, the man who could give her family the peace they deserved. And as she stared into his eyes the world seemed suddenly to make sense.

Luca held all the answers.

'Yes.'

The single word simultaneously excited and terrified her. Reeling from her boldness, she made a mental dash for the safety rope, for the back-up chute that must surely be there. But something in his eyes pulled her back, something in the way he held her kept her there, until all she cared about was here and now and not letting this moment end.

And as he thrust inside her, as she welcomed him shamelessly into her sweet oiled warmth, her words were a needless affirmation, her consent already irretrievably delivered.

'Yes, Luca, I'll marry you.'

CHAPTER FOUR

'HAVE a drink.' Luca smiled, his hand resting on Felicity's thigh as she gazed out of the window. A lump surely as big as the book she'd been pretending to read swelled in her throat as the plane lifted up into the sky, the dimmed cabin lights providing a welcome moment of privacy as she contemplated all she had left behind. 'I'm sure they can rustle up a couple of vodka and oranges—even a strawberry daiquiri…' His voice trailed off as the cabin lights flicked on, and he started in concern as he saw her stricken face. 'I was joking,' he said. 'Just trying to make you smile.'

'I know,' Felicity admitted, picking up a serviette to blow her nose and then changing her mind. Gone were the days of economy class and paper napkins. Settling for the heavy silk handkerchief Luca pressed into her hand, Felicity blew rather loudly. Luca's rather startled look caused a reluctant smile to shine through her pain. 'It's just hard, leaving them behind.'

'But you are not leaving your family behind. You can fly back tomorrow—next week if you choose. The world's a tiny place; you're only a day and night away.' His voice grew more solemn. 'I'm not going to keep you from your family, Felice. I know how important they are.' She nodded, but tears were too close to permit words, and the last thing she wanted to do was cry in front of Luca again.

'As soon as I am back at work I will speak with my

lawyers and arrange for the resort to be transferred back to your father. It might take a while, though.'

Felicity looked up sharply. Eternally suspicious, she narrowed her eyes as Luca, for the first time since their meeting, seemed to be stalling for time. But Luca moved quickly to reassure her.

'You know what lawyers can be like. Nothing happens quickly these days. Surely you know my intentions are true? I have given you my word.'

But was his word enough? She had nothing in writing, just pillow talk and promises. How would that stand up in a court of law?

A shrill, mirthless laugh rang out in her mind.

What court of law?

Her tiny nail scissors weren't up to Luca's red tape.

'That's not all that's upsetting you, is it?'

Felicity shrug was non-committal, as his voice dragged her out of her introspection. 'Isn't the fact I'm effectively emigrating enough to be going on with?'

'I guess,' Luca said gently. The hand that had been resting on her thigh was still there, but, turning to face her, he softly located her lashes with his free hand, his thumb brushing away a salty tear that hovered there. 'Are you remembering your brother Joseph and when you came to Rome with him?'

How did he know? How could he have known? The agony of his words was a small price to pay for the reward of his insight, but still she held back, quelled her pain and forced a tight smile. 'It's silly even comparing it; it's nothing like back then.'

'Why do you always do that?' Luca asked, his voice serious, eyes questioning. 'Why do you always push me away?'

'I'm not.' Felicity shook her head firmly, willing him

to change the subject. It was a bone of contention between them lately. Luca, now he had a ring on her finger, assumed he should be privy to her innermost thoughts, but Felicity consistently refused to go there.

Her innermost thoughts were not really up to an open inspection from Luca.

'You never let me in—never let me know what goes on in that ordered mind of yours,' Luca pushed. 'You're so damned independent. You never let me know what you are really thinking.'

'I'm not holding back from you,' Felicity said firmly. 'Believe me, there's really nothing very exciting going on in there.' Tapping the side of her head, she gave a tight shrug, picking up the menu the steward had handed her and pretending to read. She tried to immerse herself in the delicious delicacies on offer but it was all to no avail when the only delicacy she craved sat not a breath away. 'It's just hard saying goodbye to my family…'

'Am I not your family now?' Still his hand was on her cheek, hot and warm and infinitely strong. 'Can't I make you happy?'

Oh, how she wanted to lean against him, to bury her head in that strong, strong shoulder.

How badly she wanted to believe him.

But how could she?

Every push for information, every attempt to rationalise things, to draw up some sort of guideline, a blueprint for their marriage, had been rebuked with a familiar flick of his wrist. Every attempt to work out where she stood shrugged off.

'Details?' Luca would say. 'I'll take care of all that. Just enjoy now.'

But now wasn't enough. A taste of paradise had left her hungry for more.

The questions were becoming more insistent now. Oh, Luca had been true to his word—since the night of the awards she hadn't even laid eyes on Matthew, just heard the excited chatter of the hotel staff about his undignified exit, and even though it was what she had wanted, secretly dreamed of, still it unnerved her.

Matthew had had a contract, shares, a token holding in the company—yet it had proved nothing against the might of Luca.

What did she have?

She glanced down at the massive diamond of her ring, glinting back at her, soothing her momentarily, distracting her from the impossible conundrums that taunted her mind. For all Luca's supposed poor taste, the ring he had chosen for her was just exquisite, a massive single pear-shaped diamond set high on a claw setting. The simple fine gold wedding band was almost obliterated by the sparkle of the stone.

Surely it counted for something?

'Talk to me, Felice,' Luca grumbled. 'I hate flying.'

'I'm tired, Luca.' Felicity sighed, resting back in her seat and closing her eyes, desperate for two minutes' peace, for a chance to gather her thoughts into some semblance of a shape, to wade through the mass of emotions that seemed to be suffocating her.

Being married to Luca was exhausting.

Wonderful, exciting, exhilarating—yes.

But still exhausting.

Life with Luca was a constant rollercoaster ride, his volatile nature unreadable at times, but Felicity was slowly working it out. Sulking moods culminated in huge rows which invariably ended up in bed. He simply couldn't comprehend that Felicity might actually like her own company now and then, might need ten minutes in the bath without him joining her, might want to read a book without discussing the entire plot along the way.

It was like living with a spoilt two-year-old, Felicity thought with a surge of spite that surprised even herself. Yes, like trying to cope with a spoilt two-year-old *and* a demanding newborn, if you factored in his rather impressive manhood, that awoke at all hours waiting for attention and very loudly making it known that until it was satisfied no one in the room was going to get any sleep!

Her spite was short-lived. As his hand lazily stroked her thigh it took all the restraint she could muster to hold her relaxed pose, to quell the bubbling cauldron of emotions that Luca so easily aroused.

Luca wanted no more than she did.

She didn't want her own company right now, didn't want to lie in the bath alone when Luca was just a room away—and what was the point of reading when Luca was the book she lived by, when he was her beginning, middle and end?

'You've never told me what happened to Joseph.'

Flicking her eyes open, Felicity let out a weary sigh and again focused her attention on the menu. But when he took it out of her hands she realised Luca wasn't going to be brushed off. He carried on with this most painful subject. 'It would seem to be a no go area with your father?'

Felicity nodded. 'He gets upset if we talk about it. He says talking won't bring him back.'

'Talking is good,' Luca said gently. 'Why don't you try?'

Automatically she went to shake her head, to retrieve her menu and dismiss his offer. But when she briefly looked up the eyes that met hers were so steeped in concern, so infinitely understanding, her dismissal died on her lips. Despite her initial annoyance, deep down she was grateful. Grateful for Luca's insight, for his persistence.

Grateful to have someone to lean on, however fleetingly.

'He died in Rome.' The silence that followed wasn't uncomfortable and, Luca held her hand as she struggled to find words to sum up the most difficult part of her life. 'Joseph had a melanoma.' She registered his frown. 'A form of skin cancer. He'd had it for a while, but things seemed to be going well—the doctors said he was in remission, said that he was over the worst. They were wrong.'

She swallowed hard, taking a moment to sip her water before carrying on. 'There really wasn't much they could do for him. We tried everywhere, but each time the answer was the same: enjoy what time he's got. Then I found out about this treatment in America—but, like I said, it was never about curing him.'

'This is why your father sold the resort?'

Felicity nodded, but, registering the guilt flickering across his face, she knew more needed to be said. 'You weren't to know, Luca,' she said softly.

'Maybe, but the truth is it never felt right. When it came on the market Matthew brought it to my attention. He was an assistant manager at my Melbourne hotel, and when he first suggested I look at it I had this idea that business clients who were staying for a few weeks in Australia could go there at weekends—have a bit of a break from a formal hotel, take in some golf and tennis. It was just a germ of an idea, I wasn't even really sure I wanted to take on the resort, so I put in a ridiculously low offer—expecting, of course, some negotiation—but when my first offer was accepted, naturally I went ahead.'

'It was business.' There was no bitterness in her voice now, just a weary acceptance of the facts. 'Dad should have held out for more, but he was desperate to free up some money. It had been on the market for months without a single offer.'

'If only I'd known.'

Felicity shook her head. 'You're a businessman, Luca, not a charity. You did nothing wrong—I can see that now.' She was speaking the truth. The benefit of hindsight, hearing Luca's take on things, watching the way he ran his business, had cleared up so many of her misgivings. 'Anyway, Joseph went to America with his girlfriend and had the treatment, and when he came back we barely recognised him.'

'He was worse?'

'Oh, no.' He watched a smile break over her face like the morning sun rising above the mountains in his beloved village, and he found himself smiling back as she spoke. 'It was like getting him back. He went to America so weak and ill, a shadow of the man we all loved, but when he came back… Oh, Luca, he'd put on weight and he had this energy, this vitality, this thirst for life. It was so wonderful to see. Dad was right to sell; it was worth every last cent to get Joseph back for a while. He used every moment, lived each day as if it was his last. Kate, his girlfriend, took him to Paris…'

He watched the smile fade from her face and ached to put his arms around her, to somehow shield her from the pain to come. But a deeper instinct told him to wait and he sat quietly, holding her hand as she told her story and the plane sliced through the night sky, trapped in their own time capsule, happy to escape from the world awhile.

'Kate had to get back to work. It was supposed to be a short holiday, but Joseph got it into his head he wanted to see Rome. He was very artistic.'

'Are you?'

Felicity gave a soft laugh. 'Not in the slightest. I wish I was, but even with the best will in the world "artistic" isn't a word that would describe me.'

'Doesn't matter. Perhaps you're more…' Smiling, he shook his head, willing the word that would describe her to come to him. But somewhere high over the hot red earth of central Australia everything stilled for a second, and the low hum of the engines was the only sound as he realised his lack of eloquence had nothing to do with the language barrier that sometimes thwarted him, and everything to do with Felicity. Nothing about her could be summed up in a single word; nothing about her could be relegated to a single sentence.

'You're just you,' he finished lamely. 'So—you came to Roma with Joseph?'

Felicity nodded. 'It was wonderful. We visited the galleries, the Colosseum, the Vatican.' Her eyes shone as she spoke. 'We sat out on the pavements drinking coffee…'

Luca gave a tight smile. 'It might be a bit cold for that at the moment. What else did you do?'

'All the touristy things—ate gelato, threw coins in the Trevi Fountain.' Her smile faded, pain clouding her eyes as she carried on talking. 'Joseph wouldn't throw one in. Our guide said that if you throw in a coin…'

'You will return to the eternal city,' Luca finished softly.

'Joseph said it was a wasted wish.'

'But you obviously did?' Luca smiled.

'I threw in three. The guide said, "One to return, two to marry an Italian..."' A blush crept up her cheeks and she shook her head in bewilderment, the innocent gesture taking on an entirely new slant now. '"Three to live happily ever after."'

Luca gave a low laugh. 'There are many different versions of the legend. The one my mother always told us was "one to return, two to marry, three for a divorce."'

He always did that, Felicity thought with a pang of clarity. Every step forward that they took together Luca instantly depleted with two rapid steps back. Every glimmer of intimacy was shrouded by their inevitable departure—almost as if he'd changed his mind midway, as if suddenly she bored him.

'What happened then?'

She dragged her mind back, forced herself to the conversation, but the see-saw of emotions he provoked was too much for her now, his thoughtless comments, his deliberate withdrawal shattering any bridges they might have built.

'He died, Luca.' Retrieving the menu, she ran her eyes down it, painfully aware of his bemused eyes scorching into her cheeks. 'That's all you need to know.'

'Once we get there you will feel better.' His attempt to comfort her had an almost patronising ring, and Felicity bit back a smart reply as he carried on assuredly. 'When we arrive in Rome my driver will collect us and take us to my village. Everyone is very excited to meet you.'

'You've got two sisters and two brothers?' Felicity checked, glad of the change of subject and doing a quick mental calculation to work out the size of the entourage that would surely greet them.

'And their children, of course. And then there will be my cousins and aunts and uncles.' He managed a nervous swallow before continuing. 'And I think my mother has invited a few family friends.'

'Anna?'

Luca nodded. 'With Ricardo.'

'Not exactly an intimate dinner party, then?'

'Not exactly,' Luca conceded. 'But we won't have to stay too long. Once we have had a few drinks and said hello I will take you to our home.'

Our home.

He made it sound so simple, as if they really were two normal newlyweds crossing the threshold of their new lives together, sharing a home, dreams, aspirations.

'I'm looking forward to that,' Felicity admitted. 'Maybe once we're there it will seem more real. The hotel was nice and everything, but it will be lovely to finally be just the two of us. I can't believe I'm actually looking forward to doing housework again!'

'Scusi?' Luca gave her a horrified look. 'You won't have to lift a finger. There are staff to take care of all that.'

Sinking back in her seat, Felicity let out a low sigh. She was sick of staff—sick of being taken care of. She wanted Luca to herself, wanted time alone with the man she loved.

Loved.

How easily the word popped into her mind, but how terrifying the consequences.

She had loved him from the moment she met him, had recited her vows with an honesty that petrified her, but Luca didn't want her love. Luca wanted a temporary solution, with honour the only vow they had privately agreed to keep. Luca wanted a wife he could eventually discard with ease, and love simply didn't factor into their marriage.

That secret was hers to keep.

'Rosa might be a bit of a problem.' Luca broke into her tortured thoughts and gave a half-laugh, more to himself than to Felicity. 'She is my housekeeper; she has been in the family years. She always gives…' His voice trailed off and he looked uncomfortable as Felicity finished his sentence for him.

'Your girlfriends a hard time? You can say it, Luca. I know full well I'm not the first woman to share your bed.'

'I'm sorry,' he mumbled. 'Anyway, she'll come around in the end. Although tact isn't her strong point. If you think I put my foot in it often, just wait till you meet Rosa.' He winced slightly as he looked over. 'She'll probably call you Anna. She won't mean it, it's just that she gets mixed up. She's getting older.'

'I get the picture, Luca.' Felicity sighed. 'This isn't going to be as easy as I thought.'

'Nonsense,' Luca said quickly. 'Felice you will be wonderful—they are all going to love you!'

'I don't even speak Italian,' Felicity pointed out unnecessarily. 'And you've told me that hardly anyone speaks English.'

'Anna and Ricardo do.' Luca's attempt to soothe her didn't fare particularly well, and the involuntary look she shot at him had even Luca shrinking back in his seat a touch.

'Surely you can manage a few words of Italian by now?' Luca nudged her. 'You must have picked up some in our two weeks together.'

'A few, I guess.' Her lips twisted into a devilish smile. 'But I'm sure they shouldn't be repeated.'

He actually blushed. Leaning over, he whispered into her ear, his hot breath causing a shiver to ripple through her. 'That, *bella*, is for your ears only.'

'I hope so.' The words were out before she could stop them; she watched him frown, heard his intake of breath and wished she could take them back.

'What is that supposed to mean?'

'Nothing.' Felicity shrugged, keeping her voice deliberately light. 'Anyway, the only two Italian words I really know are *caffè* and *latte*, which is exactly what I fancy right now!' Pushing the call button, she ignored the tightening of his hand on hers, the hurt questioning look in his eyes. But Luca refused to be fobbed off.

'Felice, I would never deliberately hurt you. Surely you know that much?'

The flight attendant was there, smiling her pussycat smile as she moved the blanket an inch tighter around Luca's knees. As naturally as breathing he moved forward, giving her room to plump his pillow, and it dawned on Felicity then that it wasn't just the fact he was a first-class passenger that instigated this response. Hell, *her* blanket was somewhere mid-calf right now, and no one seemed to care! It wasn't even Luca's rather arrogant assumption that every whim would be catered to; there was an aura about him, an intrinsic appeal not easily defined, and it unnerved her.

She felt as if she were emerging from a cocoon. The

last few weeks had been a whirlwind, yes, but somehow she had felt cosseted, wrapped in a safe Santanno blanket, protected from the elements by the impressive, ordered wheels of the hotel. Cars appearing from nowhere, taking them to her family. Luca taking care of every last detail. Even her own wedding had been easily arranged; all Felicity had had to do was slip on a dress and admire her image.

But now…

The safe cocoon was gone, and her first glimpse at the sun—or, more pointedly, the camera lens of a photographer at the airport—had truly terrified her. She was in Luca's world now. Very soon it would be *her* filling the social pages of the newspapers, and no doubt her unlikely status would cause more than a few caustic comments from the reporters.

Luca's world was one in which she simply didn't belong.

'Could I have a *caffè latte* please?'

'Right away.' The stewardess's smile didn't move an inch. She didn't point out that dinner would be served soon, or that there was a whole bar on offer, but the warmth reserved for Luca was noticeably absent, the feminine smile gone now. Felicity realised there and then that the curious stares directed their way all morning, the inevitable mordant words of the journalists, hadn't really been aimed at her. Her adulation for Luca wasn't exclusive; his irrefutable grace and charm didn't only work their magic on her.

It could be Audrey Hepburn sitting next to Luca, and still she wouldn't be deemed good enough!

Retrieving her own blanket, Felicity leant back in her vast seat, the glint of her diamond offering little reassurance now.

'Felice, you didn't answer me.' Luca's voice was more insistent now. 'I said I'd never deliberately hurt you.'

'Not deliberately, perhaps…'

Her coffee appeared like magic, with a couple of chocolates and some tiny almond *biscotti*—and, of course, a good splash of whisky for her favourite client's glass and another fluff of his pillow.

Felicity choked back the nauseating waft of perfume that lingered in the stewardess's wake. Staring out of the window, watching everything familiar disappear before her eyes, she felt the biggest wave of homesickness threaten to choke her, and she wasn't sure if she even voiced the words that came next. 'I've a feeling you just can't help yourself…'

CHAPTER FIVE

WALKING into the Santanno family home was, Felicity decided, rather like pressing the wrong button on the remote control and plunging, utterly unprepared, into some very exotic, extremely loud foreign movie.

Without the aid of subtitles, though!

From every angle raven or silver-haired beauties descended upon her, kissing the air around her cheeks then holding her at arm's length, running their eyes, even their hands, over her, as if she were some fabulous dress in a shop and, Felicity gathered, asking their friend, sister, cousin or mother what they thought! Thrusting plates piled with food at her, they filled her glass with a deep rich red wine which was the last thing Felicity fancied right now, but her attempts to put her hand over her glass were countered by them prising her hand away. *'Cincin,'* a very glamorous grandmother insisted, when Felicity attempted to stop them but she shook her head.

'Could I have some water, please? Water?' she repeated, in what she hoped was a friendly voice. But her patience turned to exasperation as she was met with another nonplussed look.

'She doesn't have a clue what you're going on about.'

That deep, low voice relaxed her in an instant. A glass of iced water was being pressed into her hands and Felicity took a grateful sip. 'All I wanted was a glass of water.'

'And all they want is a piece of you. I think you've proved rather a hit, Felice. They're going to monopolise you all night, I'm afraid.'

'That's fine.' Felicity smiled, and the most amazing part of it all was that she didn't mind a bit. They were loud, colourful, overbearing—but, Felicity realised almost instantaneously, just gorgeous.

'The only trouble is, if they don't even understand "water" how on earth are we supposed to communicate?'

'It has its advantages. We can talk about anything!' Luca winked. 'Just keep on smiling and they'll keep right on smiling back.'

'What's happening?' The crowd was gathering again, and a knife or spoon was clinking on the edge of every glass in the room—everyone seemed to be joining in! Her glittering eyes turned questioningly to Luca, who had never been more than an arm's length away, surveying his family with a slightly bemused smile on his face.

'It's an Italian tradition.'

'What is?'

'Every time someone chinks their glass we're expected to kiss. It will go on all night.'

'All night?'

His arms were around her, his face bearing down, and Felicity looked up shyly, expecting a brief kiss, a polite retort to the demands of the room. But as Luca's lips met hers he pulled her in so tight her breath came out in a quick, surprised gasp, instantly smothered by the weight of his lips.

As the appreciative cheers of the room faded into the distance the rough scratch of his chin surely cut her face to shreds. He moulded her body into his and claimed her in the most blatant, possessive, public display of affection.

'All night,' he said, pulling away slightly, his voice rough, his eyes dilated with lust. The scent of him was hot and sexy, his touch almost more than she could bear and still stay within the bounds of decency.

'Don't I deserve an introduction? After all, I did choose the ring!' A heaving, throbbing purr broke the moment, and with the sudden tension in Luca Felicity didn't even have to guess who the voice belonged to.

Turning, a smile painted on, she faced her predecessor, determined to play it cool, to accept Luca's past as easily as he had accepted hers. But nothing had prepared Felicity for the sheer, stunning opulence of Anna. The newspaper photo hadn't even begun to capture the magnificent curves, the ripple of black curls that cascaded down her long neck, the magnificent bosom that spilled out of her black velvet dress, the tiny waist flowing into curvaceous buttocks, mocking Felicity's own less voluptuous offerings. She felt like a pale, washed-out shadow beside this utterly ravishing creature.

'Felicity, this is Anna...' Luca didn't miss a beat, his voice didn't waver and his smile stayed fixed, but as his hand slipped from her shoulders and came to rest in the small of her back, pushing her gently forward for the awful introduction, she could feel the ball of tension in his fist. From the sudden hush in the room, Felicity knew she had every reason to be nervous.

'Pleased to meet you.'

'And Ricardo—' Luca carried on with the formalities '—Anna's husband and my very dear friend.'

'Pleased to meet you.' Felicity blinked in surprise as Ricardo Giordano stepped forward, her vision of some geriatric playboy vanishing. In his sixties he might well be, but Ricardo was one of those men who aged beautifully. His hair was for the most part silver, but superbly cut, and there was barely a line on his swarthy face. He was almost as tall as Luca, and had a deep, steady voice and come-to-bed eyes that had probably been winning women over for years.

'Bella!' There was no formal handshake this time, not even the customary air kisses Felicity was getting used to. Instead Ricardo took his time, kissing her none too discreetly on both cheeks and then her lips as Luca's fist practically indented into her back.

'You 'ave excellent taste, Luca.'

'So do I,' Anna purred, picking up Felicity's hand and taking her time to examine the ring. 'We had such a fun afternoon choosing it—didn't we, Luca?'

Her voice dropped so low it was almost baritone, and Felicity stood there bristling with indignation as Anna surveyed the diamond, a malicious smile curving her full mouth as she shot a black look for Felicity's eyes only.

'Of course Luca wanted to rush things,' she murmured. 'You know what men can be like. But I said, "No, darling, we have to take our time. I know what women want, and this is something we really should get right." And we did!' The note of triumph in her voice didn't go unnoticed, and neither did her sexual innuendo.

'Yes, you did,' Felicity said calmly, slipping closer to Luca, eternally grateful when he reciprocated with a possessive squeeze of her bare arm. 'So, thanks for your input in choosing the ring.' Placing her glass on a tray, Felicity shot Anna her own black smile. 'I'm having such fun *wearing* it!'

* * *

It should have been a wonderful night. Luca's family had pulled out all the stops, opening up their impressive home and welcoming her into the expensively scented bosom of their family, but Felicity felt as if she were trapped on a merry-go-round. The lights and the colours were all merging into one, with only one constant remaining: Anna's black eyes, mercilessly trained on her.

She wanted to push the stop button, to get off, for Luca to take her home—wherever that was—to get back some order, to establish some sort of routine. She wanted some sort of normality to prevail.

'It is hard work, yes?'

Ricardo caught her in an unguarded moment, blowing her blonde fringe skywards as she blew an exhausted sigh heavenwards.

'They're all charming,' Felicity countered, her smile snapping back into place. After all, Luca had played the part of devoted fiancé and newlywed for her family's benefit; it was only fair to return the favour. 'I'm just tired after such a long flight—although I have to admit I feel guilty complaining; we slept most of the way. I can't believe that those chairs turned into beds.'

Realising how gauche and unsophisticated she must sound, describing the wonders of first-class flying to this sophisticate, Felicity gave a helpless shrug, blushing to her roots. Ricardo merely smiled.

'Ah, but there is nothing like your own bed. Especially when you get to my age.' He flashed her a very endearing smile. 'You are not used to flying?'

Felicity shook her head, deciding there and then that she liked Ricardo. 'The occasional family holiday from

Melbourne to Queensland and one trip to Europe doesn't really compare.'

'You can soon get used to it—that is if you want to, of course.'

Ricardo read Felicity's frown, his distinguished features breaking into another smile. 'Our partners lead a jet-set existence, and it can be a bit exhausting keeping up sometimes. Me, I like to stay here, with my grapes.'

'Your grapes?'

Ricardo grinned more widely. 'They are my babies.'

He was nice, Felicity realised, and maybe—just maybe—she had got it all wrong. Ricardo was no idiot, and he was certainly a good-looking, sexy man in his own right. Maybe Anna was in love with him. But just as she relaxed, just as the night didn't seem so bad after all, every nerve shot into overdrive. Ricardo had carried on talking, his voice so casual it took a moment to register exactly what he was saying.

'I am sorry Anna upset you earlier, flirting with Luca like that. It was most inappropriate.'

'She didn't—she wasn't—' Felicity stammered. 'I mean she didn't upset me.'

'She did and she was.' He spoke with the same heavy accent as Luca, but his English was also spot-on, and Felicity lowered her eyes, unsure what to say. After all, this was Anna's husband. 'I will speak to her the second we get home. You are a nice lady, Felicity, I don't want to see you embarrassed. Anna and Luca will just have to learn to be more discreet.'

'Discreet?' Felicity shook her head in bewilderment. 'There's nothing going on.'

'Oh, Felicity...'

Recoiling from the pity she saw in his eyes, she shook her head more firmly this time. 'You've got it all wrong,' she insisted, but the doubt in her voice was audible even to herself. 'Nothing happened at the hotel—nothing at all.'

'Did Anna choose your ring?' Black eyes were testing her now, watching her every move. 'Of course she didn't. You know it and so do I. Anna's performance before was just part of the charade—the charade we all live by. But Luca is a good man, Felicity, he will never dishonour you, never cause you shame. You are his wife after all.'

Ricardo was smiling, trying to comfort her, to reassure her, but there was no comfort to be had. She felt like putting her hands up to her ears, to block out the fateful words he was uttering, to shield herself from a truth she couldn't bear to admit.

'You will have to learn to look the other way.'

'There you are.' Luca was back, only this time the sight of him did nothing to soothe her. She desperately wanted some space to think things through. 'You look tired.'

She could see the snowflakes dusting his hair, and the cool of the night air he had brought in with him made her shiver slightly. His eyes were loaded with concern, and one tender hand brushed a stray curl from her face, capturing her chin and holding it there for all the world as if he truly cared.

'I am.' Her voice was high, her heart pounding so loudly she was sure he must be able to hear it. 'Where were you?'

'Talking to my mother.' He shot her a quizzical look. 'Where did you think I was?'

'You left your drink on the balcony, darling.' Anna joined them, her deep throbbing voice grating now, and even if she had wanted to Felicity couldn't ignore the snowflakes on Anna's hair, the intimate way she handed Luca his drink and worse, far worse, the compassion in Ricardo's eyes as he flashed a wry, sympathetic smile at her.

The merry-go-round was slowing now, the colours and the lights separating. the world was coming back into sharp focus and Felicity didn't like what she saw. 'Take me home, Luca.' Her voice was a mere croak, and if the floor hadn't still been spinning under her she'd have refused the arm Luca offered her, refused the shred of support he offered and walked out of the room unaided.

'Ricardo says that you and Anna need to be more discreet.' They were driving up and up. The winding roads were carved into the mountainside, the precarious drop visible in the pale moonlight. But even driving on the 'wrong' side of the road at a seemingly alarming speed didn't faze her. Her mind was still reeling from the little gem Ricardo had so readily imparted, wondering how best to play this. Stealing a look sideways, she drank in the haughty profile that still made her catch her breath, the straight roman nose, the sculpted cheekbones accentuating his almond-shaped eyes, and wished, now more than ever, that his beauty didn't touch her so.

'Ricardo doesn't know what he's talking about.' Shifting gear, he fiddled with the radio, obviously not remotely bothered by the conversation. But Felicity badly wanted answers.

'He seems pretty sure. Look, Luca, I know this isn't a conventional marriage, and I know this isn't going to last for ever, but I will not be made a fool. I can't bear the thought of you leaving her bed and coming to mine.'

The idle drumming of his fingers on the steering wheel only incensed her further.

'Luca, will you damn well listen to me?'

'When you have something relevant to say, then I will listen,' he responded haughtily.

'Oh, this is extremely relevant. ' Her hand shot to the radio, flicking off the opera. She was determined to force his attention. 'Do you intend to carry on as before with Anna?'

'Before what?' he asked rudely.

'Before we were married,' Felicity said through gritted teeth. 'Do you intend to have her as your mistress?'

'Why would I need a mistress?' His hands flew off the wheel, his outstretched palms gesticulating wildly in the air, and Felicity's hands gripped tighter on the seat as she debated the wisdom of confronting him as the car hugged the mountainside. 'As long as I'm with you there is no need.'

'Is that a threat?'

A long hiss of breath was the only answer forthcoming.

'Do you mean that as long as I keep coming up with the goods you'll stay away from Anna? That the second I don't toe the line and fall into your arms you'll find solace in Anna's?'

'You are twisting my words.'

'Oh, I don't think so, Luca. You told me you were talking to your mother.' She could hear a needy note creeping into her voice and fought quickly to check it. 'Instead you were out on the balcony in the freezing snow doing heaven knows what with Anna.'

He didn't answer, just carried on driving, his face set in a grim line.

'I will not be made a fool of, Luca. If something is going on between you two then I want to hear it from you. Anna said—'

'"Anna said!"' He spat the words out '"Ricardo said!"' The car swerved momentarily but he quickly controlled it, the lapse in concentration doing nothing to improve his temper. 'I am your husband, for God's sake,' Luca shouted. 'Doesn't what *I* say surely count for more? Why do you listen to them? Why do you believe them and not me?'

'Because…' She tore her eyes away. The sheer drop outside her window was preferable to the torture of looking at him, seeing his charitable smile if she dared tell him the truth. That this was not nor had it ever been a mere solution. That this marriage wasn't one of convenience, in fact it was a terrible inconvenience. It had turned her world upside down. She'd follow him to the other side of the earth just to be near him. All that sustained her was the blissful thought of being made love to by him, held by him, cherished by him.

The car was crunching along gravel now, then screeching to a halt outside a massive stone building. Lights flicked on as Luca pulled on the handbrake, his ragged breaths growing more angry now.

'My father smokes; my mother does not like him to do it indoors.' His voice had a patronising ring to it, as if she were suffering from some sort of delusional paranoia that he refused to go along with. 'That is why we were outside; there is nothing more sinister to it than that. And,' he added nastily, 'if you'd bothered to come out and join your husband, instead of sulking inside and hanging onto Ricardo's every word, we wouldn't even be having this discussion.'

'So I've got it all wrong?' Felicity retorted with a sarcastic sneer. 'Or perhaps I've got it all right. I just didn't "look the other way" quickly enough.'

An elderly couple was bearing down on them now, the man pulling open the boot, the woman shivering expectantly in the snow like a dog greeting its master after a long separation.

'I suppose this is the infamous Rosa?'

'She will be looking forward to meeting you.'

'I must remember that when she calls me Anna,' Felicity snapped. 'And I expect you want me to switch into dewy-eyed newlywed mode now—after all, it wouldn't do to disappoint the staff.'

Luca let out a low hiss. Wrenching open the car door, he walked around the front, forcing a greeting to the elderly couple who rushed over to greet them, his breath white in the cold mountain air. Felicity sat shivering, the icy cold air blasting in through the open door preferable to the cold black stare that greeted her as Luca wrenched her own car door open.

'Come on, darling.' His voice was like a caress, but Felicity was privy to the blind fury in his eyes. 'I can't wait to get you inside.' In one lithe movement, ignoring her indignant wail of protest, he scooped her into his arms, angrily kicking the door closed with one very well-shod foot and fixing his bride with a menacing smile as he bundled her against him. He carried her up the steps with barely a breath, and through the front door for her first glimpse of her marital home, barely in focus as Luca marched purposefully through the hallway and the line of staff looked on with wide smiles.

'Put me down, Luca.' Her voice was soft, her forced smile staying in place but her eyes letting it be known she meant business.

'When I am ready. As you said, we must not disappoint the staff.'

'Luca—' Still her voice was calm, but her anger was starting to mount; she utterly refused to be intimidated by him. 'If you don't put me down this instant I'll blow this little charade out of the water.' She knew she wasn't going to win, knew the arms wrapped tightly around her would only let her go when he was good and ready, and she also knew that the delicious wide mouth would silence her in a second if she registered her protest.

Well, two could play at that game!

Boldly she pressed her mouth against his, registering his gasp of surprise as her tongue edged his lips apart. As their mouths entwined his grip tightened, his breath coming faster at her audacious response, his eyes closing involuntarily as he soaked in her delicious scent, but opening abruptly when Felicity pulled away.

'Now will you put me down?'

For once he did as requested, but as he gently lowered her she almost wished he hadn't, secretly missing the strength he had imbued her with as she faced the suspicious, curious looks of the gathered entourage, and beating back a beastly blush as Luca introduced her in rapid Italian.

'This is Rosa and Marco.' He guided her forward, and even as she put out her hand to shake Rosa's she instantly regretted her rather formal greeting.

'You're supposed to kiss her on the cheeks,' Luca said in a low voice, but his warning came too late, and as the elderly woman's hand reluctantly shook

Felicity's she realised there and then that she had already lost a few Brownie points, that the rather proprietary Rosa wasn't the sweet old lady Luca had so happily described.

'Come.' With something akin to a sniff she led them through to what Felicity assumed was the lounge, though the high walls and dark leather furniture, the cool marble of the floor and the ornate antiques that lined the massive occasional tables were a million miles from the soft, welcoming lounge of her parents.

Through heavily lidded eyes he watched her, something akin to a smile softening his features as she hesitantly worked the room.

The kitten was gone. Instead she reminded him of a cat now, Luca thought. Some gracious elegant feline, with suspicious, mistrusting eyes, a proud aloofness belying her fear, choosing her seat with the utmost caution; ready to pounce, to up and leave at the slightest provocation.

'Here.' As Rosa pressed a glass into her hands Felicity eyed the pale lemon drink with caution.

'Limoncello.' Luca smiled. 'It's sweet and warm—just the thing for a cold night.'

Taking a grateful sip, Felicity nearly spat out the revolting mixture, screwing up her face and swallowing the strong sweet liquor as if she were forcing down medicine—to Rosa's obvious annoyance.

'You no like?' she asked accusingly, and Felicity shrugged helplessly.

'I'm sure it's lovely, but I would think it's an acquired taste.'

'A simple yes or no would have done.' Luca laughed as Rosa took the drink, returning almost immediately with a glass of water which Felicity accepted gratefully.

'I am sorry.' Rosa shrugged, but the smile of acceptance died on Felicity's lips as the elderly woman continued. 'It is just that Signorina Anna always likes a glass of *limoncello* before she goes to bed.'

'Ignore her.' Luca laughed again as Rosa left the room. 'She hates change, but she'll soon come around. Anna let her get away with murder, which is why she misses her so much.'

'What sort of murder?' Felicity asked, curious despite herself, her ears still ringing from Rosa's spiteful words.

'Rosa likes the *limoncello* too. When Anna was around no one really noticed the ever-decreasing bottles. I think she misses her ally.'

'And you don't mind?' Felicity asked, smiling now despite herself. 'Most people would hate their staff helping themselves to the drinks.'

'It is no big deal to turn a blind eye. Rosa is a good woman; you'll see that for yourself soon enough.'

'Well, I won't hold my breath! I'm sure Rosa's adorable where you're concerned, Luca, but I doubt that goodwill is going to extend to your wife.'

'I'm sorry for what Ricardo said.'

Felicity gave a tight shrug.

'He judges everyone by his own rules.'

'Does he have a mistress?' Felicity asked, wide-eyed, but Luca shook his head.

'Ricardo is in poor health now. I expect he has enough trouble keeping up with Anna, let alone a mistress. But with his last wife he did.'

Felicity gave a weary sigh; it was all too damned complicated for her.

'You are exhausted,' Luca said gently. 'Come, I will take you upstairs.'

She went to stand, only Luca beat her to it, and this time when he swooped her up in his arms she offered no resistance. This time she let her body curve into him, rested her head on his strong chest as he carried her up the impressive staircase, kicking open the bedroom door with his foot and gently lowering her onto a massive wooden bed.

'Poor Felice,' he whispered tenderly as with infinite tenderness he undressed her, caressing her aching feet as he pulled off her heels. 'My poor baby, it is all so confusing for you.' Massaging her shoulders, he slipped the straps of her dress down and removed her bra with all the skill and precision of a man who knew what women wanted. And while it was reassurance Felicity craved, not endearments, and though the row still resonated in her mind, it was so much easier to take the comfort Luca offered, to drown in the only succour available, to die a little in his arms as he held her.

To silence her fears with his touch.

CHAPTER SIX

'WHAT are you doing today?'

'Studying,' Felicity said determinedly, ignoring the black look Rosa flashed at her as she wandered into the kitchen in her short robe, her blonde hair tumbling. Luca rushed around, gulping down impossibly strong coffee and trying to load his briefcase at the same time. 'I'm already seriously behind. What time do you think you'll be back?'

'Late.' Luca pulled a face. 'I shouldn't ask you to wait up for me, really, but if you knew how adorable you looked this morning you'd understand why I am being so selfish.'

'Luca,' Felicity admonished, rolling her eyes towards Rosa and brushing aside his intimate observation. Luca, used to servants, didn't give a damn who was in the room, didn't lower his voice or alter his comments one iota, while Felicity felt as if she were in a perpetual restaurant—lowering her voice each and every time a waiter appeared, pausing in conversation when a napkin was placed in her lap.

And it irritated the hell out of Luca.

'Why don't you come?' he suggested 'Come on—you could do some shopping and meet me for lunch. You must be sick of being cooped up here.'

'I need to study, Luca.' Selecting a pastry from the plate Rosa pushed towards her, she took a half-hearted bite. A sickly sweet pastry was the last thing she felt like right now, but it was that or choosing from the massive tray of salami and ham Rosa always prepared, and the sight of it this morning literally turned her stomach.

'You no like?' Rosa asked accusingly.

'It's lovely,' Felicity said brightly, taking what she hoped was a more enthusiastic bite, determined to hit the local shops and find the Italian equivalent to cornflakes. A cup of tea wouldn't go amiss either, she thought, taking a sip of the strong, sweet coffee that Italians seemed to survive on.

'Can't you give the books a miss for once?' Luca pushed, but Felicity shook her head.

'I have to work, Luca; I've got an assignment due in next week. You know how important my studies are.'

Or had been, Felicity mentally corrected. The assignments that waited for her upstairs were nowhere near as inviting as a shopping spree in Rome, but she hadn't been lying when she'd said her studies were falling seriously behind and it unnerved her. She missed the safety net of lectures, the rigid timetable of university. Studying by correspondence, it was all too easy to put things off—particularly with a distraction as gorgeous as Luca. Night after night he would arrive home late, uncork a bottle of red wine and sigh with impatience as she tapped away on the computer, or run himself a long bath and then invite her to join him…

A date with her books was long overdue.

'You could bring your laptop.' Luca's voice was more insistent now. 'There's nothing you can do here that can't be done there. Come on, Felice. We could stay overnight; I'll finish work around six and we can actually have an evening together.'

The phone was ringing in the hall, and though she'd

clearly rather have stayed Rosa reluctantly went to answer it as Luca grew more insistent.

'Go and grab your books and computer and get dressed.' He gave a low laugh. 'Or on second thoughts come just as you are.'

His hand toyed with edge of her robe, melting her resistance like ice cream in the sun. Taking a deep breath, she nodded, rewarded tenfold by the smile he returned.

'It will be nice to have some time together at last.'

'We're going to be working,' Felicity pointed out, but she knew what he meant. The prospect of lunch, dinner and breakfast with him caused a bubble to well in her stomach just at the thought. Her abhorrence of hotel life seemed to have vanished after a fortnight practically alone in the house with Rosa. Moserallo was beautiful, but tiny. She'd explored every last street, walked for hours along the winding paths, attempted to chat with the locals, but without Luca she always felt as if she were just killing time, filling in the long empty hours between dawn and midnight, and the prospect of a full evening alone with him stretched before her like a delicious treat. A night in his arms with no beastly helicopter swooping out of the sky and plucking him away at some ungodly hour in the morning. 'Still, I'm sure we can squeeze in a lunch break.'

'Morning coffee too,' he whispered, his sensual mouth nuzzling the edge of her ear. 'And how about afternoon tea?'

'That's English.' Felicity giggled. 'I thought the Italians had siestas.'

'Even better.'

'Signore.' Rosa was back from the telephone and Felicity pulled away hastily, her cheeks scorching as

the elderly woman eyed her disapprovingly. *'Signorina Anna e al telefono, desidera parlare con Lei.'*

'Anna is ringing from the hotel?' Even with her non-existent Italian, the combined words of 'Anna' and 'hotel' made the message pretty clear. The fact that Anna was on the telephone at this ridiculous hour had all Felicity's senses on high alert, but she watched Luca's reaction with relief—he rolled his eyes.

'Ricardo is only letting her stay there two or three days a week now,' he offered by way of explanation. 'She will already be working.'

'She sleeps at the hotel?'

'Of course.' Again he rolled his eyes. 'I am the only fool making the journey each day. We leave in fifteen minutes.' Luca smiled, grazing her cheek with a kiss before calmly following Rosa down the hall, completely unaware of the utter chaos about to let rip in his ordered, tidy bedroom.

Felicity's reflexes were like lightning. Taking the stairs two at a time and entering the room, she flicked on her heated rollers, then made a vague attempt to gather up her books. But good as her intentions were, Felicity knew there wasn't a hope in hell of getting any work done. With Luca in the same building, concentrating on the finer points of Strategic Management or trying to wrestle with Organisational Analysis would no doubt prove an impossible feat. But, perhaps more to the point, never when she had accepted his offer had it even entered her head that she might be seeing Anna. God, she wished she had hours to tart herself up. Images of sleek Italian beauties, brimming with fashion sense, sent her into a momentary spin of panic as she waded through her wardrobe, praying for some sort of divine intervention—or at the very least a good hair day.

A smart navy trouser suit normally reserved for interviews was the best she could come up with. A touch too formal for studying, perhaps, but Felicity consoled herself that she was going to one of the most glamorous hotels in Rome—she could hardly rock up in jeans. Slipping on some heels while simultaneously brushing her hair, she abandoned all hope of a meeting with her rollers as she heard the sound of the chopper revving up in the distance—no respecter of the fashion crisis going on just a stone's throw away. The best she could hope for now was a massive squirt of gel and a prayer that the slicked-back look wasn't a complete fashion *faux pas*.

'Felice.'

She heard her summons, but ignored it, scrabbling instead in her bag for some eyeliner, pinching some colour into her pale cheeks, then rougeing her full lips.

'Felice!' She heard impatience in his tone now; standing back, she caught her reflection in the full-length mirror, admiring her handiwork as she stared at the sleek, sophisticated woman that smiled back at her.

'Felice!'

Picking up her bag, she stood at the stop of the stairwell, watching quietly for a second as he paced up and down the impressive hallway, glancing furiously at his watch as he shouted into his mobile phone.

'Was that the third and final call?'

He turned, glancing up impatiently and beckoning her with his free hand, but somewhere mid-gesture he stopped, the rapid Italian fading as he bade a hasty goodbye. Clicking off the mobile, he stood perfectly still, engulfing her with the intensity of his stare, a muscle twitching in his face as she slowly walked down the stairs towards him.

'You look...' He swallowed hard as she joined him, the heady fragrance of her perfume reaching him before she did, a precursor of the delicious parcel of sophisticated femininity that tentatively joined him. 'You look beautiful,' he said simply, taking her hand as they stepped out into the crisp morning air.

'Signora.' Rosa ran up behind them and Felicity turned in surprise, the elderly lady initiating a conversation was something of a novelty. 'You no finish your pastry.'

'Oh.' Felicity glanced down at the curling pastry Rosa had wrapped in a serviette, the yellow custard oozing out of the sides, and felt her stomach tighten. 'Thank you, Rosa.'

'Breakfast on the go,' Luca said dryly. 'Come on, Felice.'

Felicity had never been on a helicopter before, and as Luca took her hand she gave a gurgle of excited laughter. They ducked, running under the blades, the false wind catching in her throat, and Luca nonchalantly climbed in, then took her hand and hauled her none too gallantly inside.

It would have been too obvious to get out her mirror, but as it was still dark outside she managed a quick check of her reflection in the window as the helicopter lifted off the lawn, glad to see the hair gel she had used really was as long-lasting as the label had promised and her hair hadn't reached manic proportions yet.

'You look fine,' Luca mouthed, catching her eye as she turned from the window and making her blush as she realised she'd been caught.

But she didn't want to look fine. She wanted to look

divine, stunning, to knock everyone's fabulously expensive silk stockings off as she gracefully swept into the building.

To show Luca's world that she wasn't a complete hick.

The noise of the rotors didn't allow for much more than amicable silence, but as the sun rose over the Italian Alps and the chopper buzzed through the sky, hugging the mountain so close Felicity was sure if she opened a window and reached out she could have plucked a handful of snow from the side, the true beauty of Luca's country finally hit her.

She could see Moserallo fading in the distance—acre after acre of neatly rowed vineyards surrounding the knot of winding roads that all led to the war memorial, standing tall and proud, gazing down on the delicious landscape, a true meeting place where old men gossiped and teenagers kissed. She could see too the stone villas, nestled in the hillsides, and the white church so small now it looked like a model. She craned her neck for a final glimpse as it ebbed out of sight, finally understanding just why Luca made the journey each day, how bland a hotel must seem beside this rich, inspiring land.

'How long till we get there?' Felicity shouted, but Luca shook his head. Fiddling in the chair, he handed her a pair of headphones.

'Far more civilised than shouting.' His voice was so low and clear when she put them on that Felicity blinked in surprise as he spoke, a grin spreading across her face. There was a certain comfort to be had, a delicious sense of intimacy, as his deliciously accented voice filled her, low and rich and for her ears only. She adored hearing him speak, lived for the telephone calls he made during the day, when she would lie on the bed as his deep, sexy voice surrounded her, only this was better. So much better, she could see him, stretched before her in his leather seat, a safety belt slung around his thighs, dark and brooding and infinitely desirable.

'Say something,' she grumbled, wanting to hear him again, wanting his lyrical voice to wash over her, wanting to hear a hint of suggestion, to see the excitement in his eyes as she responded. 'Talk to me, Luca.' He must have sensed the shift in her, the gentle throb of suggestion as her eyes met his, his bold invitation to join in the game.

He flashed her a decadent smile, stabbing her with his eyes, rolling his tongue in his cheek as he looked at her thoughtfully.

'Quanto tempo finché arriviamo?'

She loved it when he spoke in Italian to her, loved the way he lowered his voice and made love to her with his eyes. She could feel her toes curling in her smart shoes, a flush of colour warming her rouged cheeks, and her tongue bobbed out on her full painted lips.

'Circa quarantacinque minuti.'

Practically jumping out of her seat as a voice that definitely wasn't Luca's filled her ears, Felicity clapped her hand to her mouth, stifling a nervous giggle as Luca grinned wickedly at her.

'According to Leo, we'll be there in about forty-five minutes. Now…' a tiny wink shuttered his eye momentarily '…what was it that you wanted me to talk about?'

Stinging with embarrassment, utterly unable to meet

his eyes, she took a hasty bite of the pastry warming in her hot hands.

Big mistake.

Suddenly the snow-capped mountains didn't look so gentle any more, and rather more alarmingly even Luca's liquid gold voice was doing nothing to soothe her as the cabin seemed to close in around her. She could feel beads of sweat trickling between her breasts, and the stuffy confines of the helicopter were positively claustrophobic as Luca's voice droned on mercilessly about air speed and wind direction.

'Luca!' Her voice was barely a croak. Running her tongue over her lips, she struggled to take deep breaths, dragging air into her lungs, forcing herself to keep her breathing even as she begged for his attention. But Luca wasn't looking at her now; instead he was busy pointing out landmarks, as if he were a tour guide. She rummaged in her bag—for what, she didn't know—and was sure that the paltry tissue she finally produced would prove woefully inadequate.

'Luca!' Her voice was more urgent now, forcing his attention, and his mouth opened in shock as he saw the state she was in. In one movement he pushed her head between her legs, calling in rapid Italian to Leo, who mercifully produced a bag as, reeling with mortification, burning with the indignity of it all, Felicity discovered at the rather late stage of twenty-six years that she didn't like heights after all!

To add to her utter humiliation, Luca completely overreacted. Gone was the smooth businessman. In a second he had snapped into over-protective parent mode, rubbing her back enthusiastically when she wished he'd let her just die quietly—in fact, if Felicity hadn't put her rather pale and shaking foot down, she was sure he'd have arranged an ambulance to meet them.

'Why didn't you tell me?' he demanded as he led her, pale and trembling, across the landing pad. The relative safety of solid ground was still unappealing, given they were on the roof of the hotel. 'Why didn't you tell me you hated heights?'

'I only just found out.' She managed a very thin, very watery smile. 'Is there anywhere I can freshen up—before we go to your office, I mean?'

But Luca wouldn't hear of it. Assuring her she looked just fine, he swept her down the hallway, determined to get her to the comfort of his suite, barely acknowledging the lift boy as he wrenched open the massive old-fashioned gates, holding her tightly as the lift took a plunge and Felicity's stomach did the same.

It wasn't the best way to meet one's nemesis.

Anna, dressed in a blood-red suit, the skirt impossibly short, showing a massive expanse of bronzed thigh, gaped in open-mouthed astonishment as Luca led her into the massive suite, thankfully bypassing the massive mahogany desk and array of leather seats and taking her through a wooden door where—heaven of heavens—a giant four-poster bed begged her to lie down. Not wanting to argue, Felicity sank gratefully into the fluffy eiderdown, willing the room to stop moving as Anna moved in for a closer inspection.

'Che c'è?'

'We will speak in English,' Luca responded tartly, which should have made Felicity cheer, but for the first time since landing in the country she would have been grateful to have him hang politeness and just talk about her in Italian. There was absolutely no desire on her part to hear in graphic detail this morning's embarrassing tale.

They nattered on for a moment and slowly the world came back into focus. Taking a grateful sip of the water Luca had poured, she sank back into the pillows, scarcely able to believe something as simple as fear of heights could have had such a devastating effect.

Utterly and completely worn out, she watched as Anna sat down beside the bed, and to Felicity's eternal disgust not even a single globule of cellulite marred those thighs as she crossed her legs and addressed Luca in a formal voice.

'I wish you'd told me you were bringing Felicity.'

Luca didn't even look up. Pulling a handkerchief from his pocket, he gently dabbed at a wayward river of mascara before responding. 'We only decided this morning.'

'Still, it would have been better if you'd told me.' Sighing deeply, Anna raked a hand through her impressive dark curls, chewing on the end of her pen with her ruby-red lips till Luca finally turned to her. 'The reason I asked you to come directly is because we've got some dignitaries from Saudi flying in. They want you to show them around the city and meet them for lunch.'

'Deal with them,' Luca said dismissively.

'They'd rather see you, Luca. They're talking about taking out a permanent rental on a couple of the penthouse suites.'

'My wife is sick and you are asking me to play chaperone to these people? Tell them to give more notice next time—tell them I am unavailable. Tell them what the hell you like. That is what I pay you for, is it not?

Now, if you would give us some privacy, I would like to see for myself that my wife is okay.'

'Can I at least say that you'll be meeting us for coffee? Perhaps we could…' Anna began, but her voice trailed off as Luca let out an acid hiss.

'When I know what is wrong with Felice,' he snapped, 'then I will decide. Engage the red light on your way out!'

Anna didn't slam the door exactly, but at the way she tossed her hair and marched across the room Felicity found she was bracing herself for a bang.

The tension in the air lifted once they were alone.

'Engage the red light?' A smile dusted her pale lips. 'What on earth does that mean?'

'That I do not want to be disturbed,' he explained. 'Which I don't.'

Struggling to sit up, Felicity took a couple of steadying breaths, realising with relief that the room had finally stopped moving. 'It's not quite your standard office, is it?' she said dryly, taking in her surroundings. 'Was the four-poster bed an optional extra?'

'Felice…' Luca sighed. 'Until I married you I practically lived here. You could hardly expect me to sleep at my desk.'

'I guess not,' she mumbled, realising how churlish she must sound, but it wasn't the grandeur of the surroundings that was eating at her now. Anna had followed them into this bedroom without a moment's hesitation, and it irked Felicity, but, pushing her misgivings to one side, she forced a smile. 'I'm feeling a lot better, Luca. If you need to meet with these people I'll be fine. I'm just going to lie here and do some reading.'

'I'm not meeting with anyone, and *you* are not going

to be reading,' Luca said tartly. 'You are not even going to open those books of yours. First you will lie here and rest awhile, and then if you do feel better you will take a gentle walk, get some fresh air. Is there anything I can get you?'

Felicity shook her head. 'You get on with your work. I'm just going to lie here.'

'No studying,' Luca warned. 'I'll pull the curtains and let you sleep. In fact, I'm going to keep your books and computer at my desk to make sure that you rest.' After pulling the curtains he fussed a couple of moments more, tucking a rug around her and collecting her bags.

'I'm sorry, Luca,' she mumbled as he headed for the door, her eyes heavy with sleep but not wanting him to go.

'For what?

'Being sick like that. Ruining our day.'

'Who said it was ruined?' he asked softly. 'It's just nice having you here. And don't worry about being sick, I'm used to it; Bonita, my secretary, is expecting, and she takes dictation with her head between her knees at the moment, whipping out little plastic bags at the most inopportune times. Still, at least that's one thing we don't have to worry about.'

Shutting the door, he left her frowning into the darkness.

Frowning into the darkness and praying it wasn't so.

CHAPTER SEVEN

'YOU look better!' Smiling as she tentatively pushed open the bedroom door, Luca clicked off his Dictaphone and came around the desk to join her.

'I feel better,' Felicity said brightly, and she was speaking the truth. An hour lying in the dark had done wonders, and after a quick freshen-up in the bathroom she was desperate to get out and do some exploring. 'In fact so much so I think I'm going to take your advice and get a bit of fresh air.'

'Good idea.' Pulling out his wallet, he selected a credit card. 'I would love to come, but I really do have to meet with these people. Just for a short while,' he added quickly. 'You could do a bit of shopping while I am tied up. I could arrange for someone to go with you.'

'Someone to go with me?' Felicity asked, bewildered.

'Katrina can take you to the shops on the Via Condotti. All the best fashion houses are there, but they won't know your face yet, and without an appointment they can make things difficult. Katrina can deal with all that. She will introduce you to them, let them know you are my wife; she can help you plan your wardrobe.'

'But I've *got* a wardrobe,' Felicity replied indignantly. 'Are you not happy with the way I dress, Luca? Are you trying to tell me that I embarrass you?'

'Of course not,' he answered, irritated. 'But you

have just come from an Australian summer to an Italian winter, and I don't recall too many woollen coats hanging in the wardrobe, or boots or gloves. Take it,' he urged, pressing the gold card into her hand. 'What is it that women say? Go and "shop till you drop".'

'Shop till I droop, more likely.' Felicity sighed. 'Look, Luca, the last thing I feel like doing now is shopping, and when—if—I decide that a new coat or new boots are in order I'll buy them myself, thank you. I certainly don't need some wardrobe consultant telling me what colours suit me best; I worked that out long ago.'

'Why do you always have to be so stubborn?' Luca admonished. 'You are the only woman I can think of who could start a row because I tell her to go clothes-shopping! Most women—'

'I'm not most women,' Felicity broke in, popping the card into his top pocket and dousing his anger with a bright smile. 'But thank you for the offer.'

'I suppose you're going to insist on paying half for lunch,' he said broodingly, which only made her smile wider.

'Stop sulking, Luca. Look, you really ought to eat lunch with these people; you know that as well as I do. Turning down that sort of clientele is hardly a wise move. And you would be turning them down,' she said quickly as he opened his mouth to argue. 'A quick morning coffee isn't really the way to do business.'

'I guess,' he muttered. 'But come with us at least. I can't just leave you on your own on your first day in Rome.'

'Why not? I'm not a baby, Luca; I can brave the streets without an escort. Anyway, after this morning's episode a heavy long lunch really isn't at the top of my agenda—and it isn't my first day in Rome. I was here with Joseph, remember?'

'Okay,' he said resignedly. 'But if you need anything, if you run into any problems and I am not here, you ring the hotel and ask to speak with Rafaello.'

'Rafaello? Is that your personal assistant?'

'No, he is far more useful than that. Rafaello is the chief concierge. There is nothing he cannot organise.'

'I'll bear it in mind.'

'So when will I see you?' Luca grumbled. 'When can you squeeze me in?'

'Tonight,' Felicity said brightly, refusing to be drawn by his sulking. 'I'll arrange dinner; just meet me back here around six.' And, kissing him briefly on the cheek, she headed out of the door.

Wincing slightly as she worked out the exchange rate, for a while Felicity wished she had taken Luca up on his offer and pocketed his little gold credit card.

'No, you don't,' she said firmly, forging her way slowly through the crowded streets, gaping in open-mouthed admiration at the ravishing women and well-groomed men, their beautiful coats trailing massive bright scarves, immaculate shoes clicking along as they shouted in their exuberant language, blowing white clouds of air as they sipped their hot coffee or chatted noisily into their mobiles.

Rome was everything she remembered and more. Somehow shopping and art melted into one. Every turn of a corner heralded a building steeped in history, hundreds of churches, each one deserving so much more than the awe-inspired glances she gave as she teetered past, her high heels no match for the cobbled streets.

Luca, as insensitive as he might have been in his

delivery, certainly had a point. Her suit, appropriate as it might be for Australia, was no match for the icy weather here. The cold literally bit into her, and she could hear her teeth chattering involuntarily as she walked along. Bypassing elegant shops with only one or two garments tastefully displayed and not a hint of a pricetag in sight, she settled for some of the rather less imposing boutiques. They might not have been Luca's idea of heaven, but for Felicity it was like stepping into paradise. It was so easy to waste the day, wandering from shop to shop, and after an age of running her hand over fine wools and beautifully cut suits she finally threw caution to the wind and took her rather less impressive navy blue credit card out of its mothballs and gave it a long-overdue workout. After all, she would be needing the clothes soon, she consoled herself. Once she had her MBA it would be Felicity taking clients out for lunch.

If she got down and did some work for the blessed thing.

Paying for her purchases, weighed down with endless bags, she pushed her pang of guilt aside. It had been ages since she'd spent a cent on clothes, ages since she'd treated herself. Anyway, she didn't have to worry about money now her parents were taken care of.

Or would be if Luca ever spoke to his lawyer.

Catching sight of a row of ties, she ran her hands over them. The silk was so heavy the ties barely moved, but one in particular caught her eye, standing out amongst the heavy checks and bold stripes, the deep sapphire-blue an almost perfect match for Luca's eyes. Its simplicity was its beauty, and on impulse she bought it, berating herself for not looking at the pricetag as the assistant boxed it, then further wrapped it in endless wads of tissue paper before placing it in small silver bag, using practically half a forest for one simple garment. For that much paper it had to be expensive.

It was.

The slightly startled look of the hotel staff as she staggered through Reception brought a rueful smile to her lips; no doubt they expected the wife of the great Signor Santanno to arrive with an entourage of assistants weighed down with the fruits of her labours.

'Signor Santanno should be back shortly,' Rafaello greeted her warmly. 'In the meantime he has asked that I ensure you are taken care of. Would you like me to send the head chef up to you, *signora*? He can take you through the menu personally; Signor Santanno mentioned you have been finding the food rather rich.'

'That won't be necessary, Rafaello,' Felicity said assuredly. 'I've got everything I need right here.'

Even the eternally impassive mask of the concierge slipped momentarily as he relieved Felicity of a bag while simultaneously clicking his fingers to summon assistance. Undoubtedly the aroma of fresh-baked bread and the chinking of bottles were out of place anywhere other than in the impressive dining room here, but Rafaello recovered quickly.

'Is there anything I can get you, *signora*? Anything at all?'

'A picnic blanket?' Felicity asked, watching his reaction closely, but this time Rafaello never turned a hair.

'Certainly, *signora*. I will have it sent to your room immediately.'

As good as his word, a picnic blanket arrived before

she had even peeled off her shoes. Shooing out the staff, insisting she was more than capable of putting away her own purchases, she set about preparing the room, laying out the blanket, buttering the bread into thick mounds, arranging the cheeses and dried fruits temptingly, and smiling to herself at Rafaello's foresight when two chambermaids discreetly knocked, buckling under the weight of a massive silver ice bucket and huge candelabra.

Rafaello was obviously a romantic!

'What's all this?' Blinking in the semi-darkness, Luca eyed the room slowly before turning his rather bemused face to Felicity.

'Dinner in Italy,' she said softly. 'Conlon-style.' Taking the lead, she sat on the rug, and after a moment's hesitation Luca pulled off his jacket and shoes and joined her. He was uncomfortable and awkward at first, but finally—along with his tie—he loosened up, accepting the cheap red wine Felicity handed him as she sipped on some sparkling mineral water.

'Tastes like mouthwash.' He grimaced. 'Where on earth did you get it?'

'At my usual deli,' Felicity laughed. 'This is what Joseph and I used to eat when we came to Rome. We couldn't afford to go to fancy restaurants for every meal, so instead we found this wonderful deli. We'd go off and have a picnic lunch somewhere wonderful—though I admit the wine is rather an acquired taste; I just stuck to mineral water.'

'Happy times?'

'Very,' Felicity said softly. Looking up, she saw him staring at her, his face softer in the candlelight, those beautiful heavy-lidded eyes loaded with surprising tenderness. 'And so is this.'

And even though the whole meal probably cost as much as a bowl of soup in Luca's dining room, if ever there was a moment of perfection in their marriage this was it. No waiters hovering, no staff wringing their hands in an effort to help. Just her and Luca and an entire evening stretching before them. Oh, she knew they had a lot to talk about, knew there was a lot of difficult ground to cover. The stalemate with the lawyers, his refusal to give her a timeline, but for a while she put the questions on hold, determined not to mar this rare moment of togetherness.

'I bought you a present.' Handing him the parcel, she watched the question in his eyes as he accepted it. 'It isn't much,' she ventured. 'I just saw it and liked it. I thought it matched…' She swallowed hard, grateful for the candlelight to soften the furious blush that scorched her cheeks. 'It matches your eyes.'

She watched as he turned it over in his hands and then slowly peeled back the mountains of paper, pulling the tie out of its box and running his fingers over it for a moment before speaking.

'It's lovely.' His voice was thick, and when he looked up Felicity was almost knocked sideways by the raw emotion in his proud, expressive eyes. 'I shall wear it tomorrow.'

'You—you don't have to,' she stammered. 'I know it's probably nothing like the quality you're used to—'

'It's perfect,' Luca broke in. 'In fact, it is the nicest present I've ever had.'

'It's just a tie, Luca,' Felicity pointed out, startled by his reaction. 'You don't have to go over the top.'

But Luca begged to differ. 'Do you realise this is the first real present a woman has ever given me?'

'Oh, come on.' Felicity laughed nervously. 'Your dressing table at home is weighed down with Tiffany cufflinks and little one-offs that only a woman could choose. I'm sure a tie is way down on your list of memorable gifts.'

'This is the only one I will remember,' Luca said fiercely. 'Yes, women have given me *gifts*, and undoubtedly they have agonised over the choice of precious metal or the wording of an engraving, and for a while maybe I was touched. But the sentiment behind the gift tends to wane when it appears on your own credit card statement.'

His voice trailed off, his gaze returning to the fabric he held in his hands, and for the first time since their meeting Felicity felt something akin to pity for him. Something in his voice, his stance, throbbed with loneliness, and she realised there and then how hard it must be for Luca at times. How hard it must be when every friendship, every relationship, both professional and personal, was dictated by his bank balance. The price he paid for adulation.

'And this is a night I will remember too.' His gaze drifted around the blanket, the foods she had so carefully chosen, each tiny jar, each taste loaded with memories, both new and old. 'Felice, there is something I need to tell you—something we need to talk through.'

Her breath seemed to be coming in hot, short bursts, trapped in her lungs as her throat constricted, her fight or flight response triggered as his hand inched over the rug to hers. She could feel it hot and dry over hers, hear the hesitancy in his voice as he spoke.

'I have not been strictly honest with you.'

It was like the executioner's axe falling. Her heart was banging in her ribcage so loudly she was sure he must hear it. The confrontation she had sought was here now, but suddenly the truth was something she wasn't sure she wanted to hear—not if it spelt the end, not if it involved the one thing she simply couldn't forget or forgive.

'Anna!'

The word that pounded in her mind spilled from his lips, and it took a second to register that Luca wasn't confirming her worst fears, that in fact Anna had pushed open the door and was standing just a few feet in front of them.

'What are you doing here?' Standing angrily, he walked over to her, running an impatient hand through his hair. 'Haven't you heard of knocking?'

'Since when did I need to knock?' Anna drawled, then, taking in the picnic blanket, formed a mocking smile on her heavily made-up lips. With one scathing look she managed to sully all Felicity had lovingly created. 'Oh, am I breaking up a little tea party? Or have the kitchen staff all gone on strike?' Not waiting for an answer, she flicked on the lights, handing Luca a small card to sign. 'I need your signature on this, darling. I'm sending Ahmett a basket of Italian delicacies.' She gave a low laugh. 'Perhaps I should order two and have one sent up here; I didn't realise people actually drank that stuff!'

Without a word Luca took the card and scribbled a message, though from the look on his face Felicity wasn't sure it would be usable.

'Ricardo just telephoned,' Anna carried on airily, not remotely fazed by the sudden drop in temperature. 'He would like you to come for dinner on Saturday.'

Luca opened his mouth to respond, but Felicity beat him to it. 'We're busy on Saturday,' she responded curtly, and if the ambience had been cool before it was positively arctic now, as Anna took the card without a word and turned on her razor-sharp stiletto. Only this time her temper didn't stay quite so well in check, and she slammed the door loudly on her way out.

Only when she'd safely gone did Felicity let out a large sigh. 'That was pleasant.' Turning, she expected an apologetic smile or at the very least a mutual sigh of relief from Luca, but if he had been annoyed before he was livid now. His mouth was set in a grim line, every muscle in his face straining as his blazing eyes turned to her.

'What the hell did you say that for?' he demanded. 'How dare you turn down a dinner invitation from Ricardo without consulting me first?'

'I *dare* because I have no desire for a night in Anna's company,' Felicity answered tartly, but her conviction wavered as Luca's fury erupted.

'So you refuse his invitation?' Luca roared. 'Ricardo is my family's oldest friend and you refuse to eat at his table?'

'I refuse to eat at his wife's table,' Felicity responded hotly. 'I refuse to be humiliated by Anna! I refuse to allow her to laugh in my face at the mockery of this so-called marriage.'

'Is that what all this is about?' He swung around, his eyes blazing. 'Are you demanding we change the rules all of a sudden? Do you want me to say I love you, Felice? Do you want me to tell you that this is for ever?' Each word was like a knife plunging into her heart; each word lacerated her with its emptiness.

She shook her head, her hands flying to her ears. Oh,

she wanted him to love her, wanted him to tell her, but not like this, never like this—some enforced declaration, a platitude to keep her quiet, a crumb to sustain her.

'Have I ever for one moment treated you with anything other than respect? Have I ever for even a second given you reason to doubt me?' He didn't give her time to answer, his fury gaining momentum with each and every elaborate gesture. 'I told you the day we met that Anna and I were finished, and you looked me in the eye and said you believed me…'

'It was easy to believe you then.' She had found her voice, shaky as it was. 'I didn't have to see her then, pawing you, making innuendoes. The red light is on, Luca. You said yourself that meant you were not to be disturbed! But it would seem those rules don't apply to Anna. Why, even Ricardo—'

'So you are listening to Ricardo now? Listening to some *puttana's* husband? A man who would rather let people think I had slept with his wife than rejected her!' The shock on her face wasn't missed, and Luca gave a haughty nod. 'That is right. These are the people you choose to listen to over your husband.'

'You're talking as if our marriage is real!' As he let out a furious hiss she retreated somewhat, shaking her head and turning to go—to where, she wasn't sure, but she had no desire to continue this explosive argument, no wish to upturn stones and expose the horrible lies that bound them. But Luca had other ideas. Pulling her back, he swung her around none too gently, forcing her attention, stabbing her with his eyes.

'Don't you walk out on me! Come and finish what you started, Felice.'

Her eyes darted nervously; she could feel the sweat

trickling between her breasts as he moved closer, his face menacing. 'I'm just pointing out that you're talking as if we're a real husband and wife, as if…' She was swallowing hard now. She'd been pushing for this confrontation but now that it was here she didn't want it—didn't want to hear the mirth in his voice, the pity when he realised she loved him, that this wasn't nor had ever been a game to her, a solution to a problem.

That it was the real thing.

'As if what?' His voice was like a whip cracking, every word so well articulated, so measured the Italian accent almost melted away.

'As if we love each other,' Felicity whispered. 'As if it's imperative that I believe you; as if you care what I think of you.'

'And just what do *you* think, Felice?' His voice was deathly quiet, but it didn't mask the danger behind it. 'What goes on in that pretty head of yours? I've tried asking nicely, tried treading carefully, but it's got me nowhere. Well, I'm through being nice. I'm through treading gently. If you've got something to say, then now would be a good time.'

'I want you to talk to the solicitor, Luca! I want you to deliver on your promise and sort out the title at the resort, and I want you to stop sabotaging any attempt I make to study.'

Letting her go, he picked up his glass, then with a howl of anger hurled it at the wall before carefully selecting another glass from the silver tray and pouring a large whisky. 'Have you finished?' Turning, he let his eyes blaze a trail across the room, his words biting her with their savagery. 'Is that all you want from me, Felice? Is that it?'

'Not quite.'

His knuckles were white around the glass, his face deathly pale and menacing as she calmly walked towards him, every calm, measured word she spoke exacerbating the tension in the room.

'There is another thing I want from you, Luca.' She was in front of him now, her stance confrontational, utterly refusing to be intimidated by this insufferable man, refusing to let him even glimpse the agony in her soul. 'I want some respect. If you can't keep your lover quiet then at least keep her at a respectable distance.'

If Felicity had possessed such a thing no doubt she would have dressed for bed buttoned up to the neck in some Victorian cotton nightdress. Certainly, from the bristling indignation emanating from Luca, had he possessed a pair of pyjamas they'd have been on also.

Instead they had to settle for opposite sides of the bed, with Felicity practically hanging onto the mattress-edge in an effort not to touch him, concentrating on keeping her breathing even as he blew out the candles and flicked off the light, utterly determined to be the first to fall asleep.

She lost by a mile.

However much Felicity wanted to believe he was pretending, somewhere between his turning off the light and his head hitting the pillow Luca fell into the deepest of sleeps, each gentle snore rippling through her, catapulting her into a fury. She wanted to dig him in the ribs, kick him, even, demand how the hell he could go and fall asleep when there were so many questions to be answered, so much unsaid.

His hand sliding across the bed, sleepily snaking around her hips, was like being branded with a red-hot poker. She didn't want him to touch her, didn't want to lose herself in his touch. The row that had blown in needed to be faced head-on, not made up in bed. He pulled her towards him, even in sleep the attraction they generated so palpable, the sexual awareness so real it was impossible to deny it. He tucked his body into hers, pulling his knees up behind her, and she lay frozen, unyielding, wondering how to explain to this impossible, difficult man what she didn't even understand herself. That her body ached for him, that even as she lay there as still as stone he moved her, that every fibre of her being screamed for him—for all of him, not this half-life they had engineered, not this shell of a marriage without commitment.

His tumid warmth was nudging her thigh now; she could feel him responding to her. One lazy hand was almost distractedly circling her stomach, then with a low grumble he pulled her closer, snaking his fingers up and cupping her breast in his hot, dry hand.

It hurt.

Wriggling slightly, she heard his low moan of protest, but the horrible nagging question that had been plaguing her was back, and no matter how she tried to ignore it, no matter how she tried to suppress it, it was here with force now, demanding she face it, stop ignoring things and deal with the problem.

'Felice?' His low sleepy moan caused her to pause momentarily as she crept out of the bed, missing the safety of his caress already.

'I'm just going to the bathroom,' she whispered. 'Go back to sleep.'

'Let's not fight.' He didn't even open his eyes, and she stood and stared at him in the darkness for a moment, wishing it was all that simple, wishing it was all so easy.

Wishing his beauty didn't touch her so.

'Come back to bed, Felice. Don't keep pushing me away.' His hand flicked out from the sheets, warm and strong, his grip possessive, pulling her towards him. His eyes had opened, and even in the darkness she could see the desire burning there.

But she couldn't do it—couldn't slip back between the sheets, into his arms, and make love as if everything was okay, when everything around her seemed to be falling apart. When the charade she was half of was unravelling at the seams.

'I need to go to the bathroom…'

'Felice…' His hand snaked around her waist and the sheet slipped away from his dark, toned body. The full beauty of his arousal caused her breath to catch in her throat, a million wrongs righted with just a fleeting glimpse of his naked splendour. 'Come back to bed.' It was an order, not a request, but delivered with such silken promise that she felt her insides turn to liquid. His hot lips nuzzled her pale stomach, his devilish tongue working its way downwards, and her eyes closed with the agony of indecision.

Oh, she wanted him, *how* she wanted him. To lie on the bed, for his skilful lovemaking to work its undeniable magic, for him to take her to that special place he had shown her, quieting the impossible conundrums stamping through her mind, for the aftermath of her orgasm to obliterate the hopeless questions that taunted her, more soothing than a pill, more toxic than any drink and more addictive than any drug.

But what then?

'Luca, no!' Felicity's words came out more harshly than intended, and her body tensed as he instantly pulled away. She was missing him already, wishing she could somehow take back those two little words, or at the very least the ferocity with which she had expelled them. 'I mean…' Her voice tailed off, the hurt in his eyes surprised even Felicity. 'I really do need to go to the bathroom.'

'I get the message, Felice. My English might not be perfect, but you've made yourself pretty clear.'

Sitting on the bath-edge, she pulled the tiny folded paper from the Pill packet, opening it up and scanning the tiny writing. How many times in the last few days had she done this? Felicity had lost count. Each time the words had offered some assurance, some ray of hope that she wasn't pregnant.

Tender breasts, labile moods, nausea; Felicity gave a rueful laugh. Three out of three so far—*of course* it was the Pill making her feel this way; according to this it might even account for her being so late.

But…

God, she hated the bold print, the thick black letters that warned missing even one tiny pill could cause pregnancy, to take extra precautions for the next couple of weeks, oh, and by the way, could she please see a doctor if symptoms persisted!

Screwing up the flimsy paper in her fist, she threw the tiny ball into the bin and then clasped her fingers to her temples. The truth was too terrifying to contemplate.

How could she tell him, when babies weren't part of the deal?

Babies had never been on her agenda.

Ever.

A whimper of fear escaped into the still night air, echoing around the high walls of the bathroom, the impossibility of the situation overwhelming her.

Suppose she could do it—suppose she could push aside her own fears, embrace the future, however unplanned. How could she possibly tell Luca when even at a stretch, this could only be called a tenuous relationship? Looking down at her flat pale stomach, she tried to imagine it rounded and swollen, heavy with a child, with Luca Santanno's child, her breasts heavy with milk. Whatever way Felicity looked she couldn't see it—couldn't see his hand there, touching their unborn baby, revelling in every little kick, facing every milestone together.

It was all too much, too soon, and just so very terrifying.

Creeping back into the bed beside him, she lay staring into the darkness. Never had she felt more alone, more scared, and never had she needed him more.

One small hand crept across the pillow, trying to turn his rigid cheek, to force him to look at her, honesty just a breath away. 'I'm sorry for before, Luca. Of course I want you; I always have.' Still he wouldn't look at her, his face set in stone, his eyes staring at the ceiling, and she did the only thing she could, to show how much she wanted him.

Pushing her face to his, she kissed his unmoving mouth, her tongue forcing his lips apart, willing him to respond, but he lay rigid beneath her. She knew she had hurt him, rejected him, and suddenly it seemed imperative she put things right, restore their closeness with the only language Luca seemed to want to speak. Her hand moved down, her boldness terrifying her. Yes, he was her husband, yes, they had made love over and over, but never had she instigated it, never in her life had she been the one calling the shots.

Inching down, she felt the soft scratch of his chest

hair thin out; she imagined the delicious snaky line of hair over his abdomen and her nervous fingers dusted it, following the trail, her breath on hold as she tentatively lowered her head, tasting the salty warmth of his skin as her tongue worked down. She could feel his arousal against her cheek, nudging, soft and hard and warm all at the same time, and instinctively she turned, ready to take him, to taste him, to revel in him. But in one swift movement his hands shot to her shoulders, pushing her back, his dark eyes blazing with contempt.

'Are you worried when pay-day comes you won't get your bonus?' he spat as Felicity reeled backwards, her cheeks stinging, every nerve burning with mortification at his brutal rejection. 'Worried if you don't sleep with the boss, he'll renege on the contract? Well, let me tell you this, Felice. I've never had to beg for sex and I don't intend to start now. I suggest you do the same.'

Reeling with humiliation, stunned by the venom in his attack, she stared into the darkness, blinking away the lonely tears as she listened to Luca's rhythmic breathing. Trying to fathom what on earth she had done and worse, far worse, what Luca was going to say when he found out.

CHAPTER EIGHT

SOMEHOW they limped along, the endless army of staff at least ensuring their rows were confined to the bedroom.

Luca, used to a multitude of people swarming around, tending to his every whim, still sucked in his breath in indignation when Felicity stopped talking mid-sentence or dropped her voice to whisper whenever Rosa the housekeeper appeared.

'She barely speaks English,' Luca hissed one morning as they glared over their coffee cups at each other. 'Yet you carry on as if you were at a funeral.'

'I feel like I'm at a funeral,' Felicity retorted. 'Have you any idea how boring it is here? It's okay for you, swanning off to work every day.'

'I thought you were busy with your precious studies.'

'My studies are important,' Felicity flared, but Luca most annoyingly just flicked his newspaper and carried on reading. 'Just because you consider women should be barefoot and pregnant in the kitchen…'

'Heaven forbid.' Luca visibly shuddered, angry eyes peering over the top of the paper. 'Could you imagine the hell a baby would add to this supposed domestic bliss?'

It wasn't a point Felicity cared to dwell on, but she was saved from answering as Rosa appeared, with the inevitable coffeepot in hand, filling his cup without waiting to be asked. Suddenly Felicity had had enough.

If Luca wanted her to carry on as normal around the staff, to say what was on her mind, then she damn well would.

'Do you realise I don't know how many sugars you have in your coffee?'

'What the hell has that got to do with anything?'

'Everything,' Felicity flared. 'You're my husband, yet I've never even made you so much as a drink. It's not just room service with you, Luca; it's a butler and waitress to boot. I've never ironed you a shirt, never cooked you dinner...'

'You're contradicting yourself,' Luca drawled. 'You were just saying before how important your studies were; now you're complaining there's not enough domestic drudgery for you. I could have a word with Rosa,' he offered sarcastically. 'I'm sure she can rustle you up a pile of dirty laundry if that's what you so desire.'

'Oh, you're impossible.' Flinging down her napkin, Felicity forced back the sting of tears in her eyes. God, he was loathsome, conceited and difficult—but she loved him. And, as boring and pathetic as it sounded, she wanted all of him, not this tiny slice she was being offered, but Luca just couldn't see it.

'I have to go to Florence today.' He was sitting reading his paper, not a care in the world, turning the pages slowly as he demolished a pastry and three impossibly strong short black coffees.

Felicity surveyed the gleaming quiet kitchen and tried to fathom Luca's take on it with a baby sitting in a high chair, throwing egg around and disrupting his much loved morning peace.

'Florence?' Felicity took a nervous sip of her *latte*, praying she could keep it down till Luca had left for work at least. She was used to the helicopter revving up around seven a.m. now, whisking him off to the Rome hotel as easily as pulling the car out of the drive, but Florence was hardly a hop and a skip away.

'I might stay the night; it depends how much work there is to do.'

'Fine.'

She could hear the chopper revving up in the distance, knew the routine already so well it hurt, but as Luca glanced at his watch and downed the last of his coffee, the very last thing she wanted was him to leave.

He gave her a vague kiss on the cheek and then, because Rosa came in, he kissed her more thoroughly, but the heavy scent of his aftershave was too much in her fragile state. As she flinched slightly she saw the start of confusion in his eyes. 'I'll ring when I get there. I'll know more then.'

'Luca?' He was at the door now, gorgeous in a dark suit, the crisp white shirt accentuating his strong olive neck, his haughty face cleanshaven, a black briefcase in his manicured hand. He looked angry and restless and confused, but infinitely beautiful. 'Have a safe trip.'

How paltry her words sounded, how utterly empty and meaningless, when the fact that she loved him was at the tip of her tongue, that she had never been more scared in her life, that today was the day she found out for sure if she was carrying his child.

He gave a stiff nod, a tight smile, but didn't say anything, and all that was left to do was sit and drink her *latte*, sit and listen to the helicopter lift into the gently rising morning sun, the whirring blades humming their own tune as he flew away.

* * *

The feel of snow crunching under her new boots was as unfamiliar as everything else, but Felicity liked it. Liked the sinking feeling as she walked along, her face hidden behind a massive wrap, her shoulders hunched in the camel-coloured coat she had bought.

She'd been offered a driver, a car, even, but to the staff's bemusement she had refused, determined to have some time to herself, to wander into the village alone and come back when she was good and ready. The mountains were amazing, everywhere she turned a picture postcard in the making—blues, greens and purples capped with snow, villages dotted like models—and Felicity took her time, stopping at the war memorial, waving to curious onlookers as they salted their paths and rushed to catch the bread van. Walking past a tiny graveyard, on impulse she wandered in. Brushing the snow off the stones with her gloved hands, she read the inscriptions. Santanno, Giordano and Ritonni appeared with alarming regularity, staring back at her like a mocking taunt again and again.

Luca, Ricardo and Anna.

Each carefully worded inscription confirmed the futility of the love triangle she had entered. Every one alienated her further, ramming home the incestuous ties that bound this town, the impossible hand she had been dealt.

This truly was Luca's territory, and never in a million years would she belong.

Even with her non-existent Italian, the word *farmacia* was pretty universal, and Felicity took a tentative step inside, relaxing as she saw the white-coated uniform of the staff. The rows of items were touchingly familiar, and she was sure she would have no trouble locating the pregnancy testing kits.

A pretty assistant smiled, offering her help, but Felicity politely declined, far happier to wander than explain what she was here for.

There they were. Congratulating herself, she surveyed the kits, looking for what she hoped would be a simple one.

'Do you know what you're looking for?'

Pulling her hand back as if she were touching hot coals, Felicity swung round aghast. 'Anna! I'm just trying to find some paracetamol. I couldn't get the staff to understand me.'

Anna frowned. 'I thought Cara spoke some English. No problem—I will show you.' She gave a low laugh. 'I hope for your sake you won't need one of these for a while. I'd hate to be the unlucky girl who tries to tell Luca he is about to become a father.'

She looked more closely at Felicity's shocked expression, thankfully misinterpreting it. 'These are pregnancy testing kits,' she explained with a throaty chuckle. 'Now do you understand what I am saying? Can you imagine Luca Santanno a father? Believe me, I know from experience it's not on his list of must-haves.' A wistful look flashed over Anna's face, and a smile bordering on sympathy flickered on her lips as she caught Felicity staring at her. 'I thought I was pregnant by the great man himself once.'

'What did he say?' Her voice was a croak. The answer was one she really didn't want to hear, but she knew deep down it was imperative she at least found out what she was up against.

'A lot.' Anna sighed, rolling her eyes dramatically.

'You know Luca; his life revolves around his work—heaven help the woman who tries to change him.'

'But what did he say about the baby?' Felicity pushed, fingers of fear wrapping around her heart as Anna's cold black eyes met hers.

'Lucky for me there was no baby, it was a false alarm. But Luca made it very clear he had no intention of becoming a father, even an estranged one. He wanted me to have an abortion,' Anna finished watching as the colour drained out of Felicity's cheeks. 'But thankfully there was no need. Let's get these tablets for you. Nothing seriously wrong, I hope?'

Felicity shook her head, still reeling from Anna's words, forcing her voice to come out even. 'I've just got a bit of a headache.'

'Oh, a headache!' The malicious smile was back. 'That's what wives get, isn't it? I must try that one on Ricardo!'

A crushing reply was on the tip of Felicity's tongue, but Anna seemed to change her mind all of a sudden, and the malicious smile was replaced by the first genuinely friendly one Felicity had seen.

'I'm joking. Come, let's get your paracetamol and I will get Ricardo's antacid. He was complaining of chest pain this morning. For a minute I thought my luck was in, but it was only indigestion.' Seeing Felicity's shocked expression, she flashed that bewitching smile again. 'You are very easy to tease, Felicity. You must toughen up a bit.'

A rapid exchange in Italian followed, and Ricardo's antacid was smothered in Anna's basket as the assistant loaded in hair conditioners, face packs and various items of make-up.

'It is so boring here.' Anna shrugged. 'Now that

Ricardo is insisting I give up work there is nothing for me to do except have facials. I understand that you and Luca were tied up last Saturday, but at the very least we should go and have a coffee—be friends. It will be nice having someone young to play with.'

Even Felicity smiled at Anna's terminology. *Playing* with Anna was way down on her list of priorities; it would only end in tears, after all! 'Maybe some other time. I really do have to get back; I'm supposed to be studying.'

'I will hold you to it. *Ciao.*' Kissing Felicity's rather taut cheeks, Anna sauntered out, spraying every perfume on display as she did so.

Only when she had gone did Felicity make her way over to where Anna had disturbed her. At least she knew she was buying the right thing now. Blushing furiously, she made her purchase, frantically trying to avoid the assistant's eyes and praying that *farmacia* staff had the same moral code as doctors, or Luca would know the answer before she did!

It was the longest two minutes of her life. Sitting in the bathroom, staring at the piece of paper, her coat discarded on the floor, her scarf still draped around her shoulders, her need to know, to be absolutely sure, surpassed everything. She was strangely calm as she awaited her fate, and the pink cross slowly appearing was not even a surprise—more a confirmation of what she already knew.

'We'll be all right.' Instinctively Felicity's hand moved to her stomach, massaging the tiny scrap of life that so clearly was meant to be. Catching sight of herself in the mirror, she wondered how she could still look the same when so much had changed. She was going to be a mother and Luca was going to be a father.

She was having Luca's baby.

It was scary and overwhelming, and everything she hadn't planned, but even in the midst of her internal chaos she could sense the beauty of the moment. Whether it was maternal instinct or just the chains of love Luca had trapped her in, she could never regret this infant for a moment, never resent a baby borne of love.

Love.

But did Luca love her?

Anna's words came back like a mocking taunt, the demons that had snapped at her heels awakening now. Her mind whirred as she played out different scenarios, tried to imagine Luca's ordered, busy life with a baby on board, a child born to a woman who was supposed to be a temporary solution.

Making her way out of the bathroom, she lay on the bed, staring dry-eyed at the small plastic indicator and the tiny pink cross that signified what she truly did not know. The beginning or the end?

'Signora?'

Even though the knock on the door was firm Felicity barely heard it, and she stuffed the indicator under the pillow, hardly even bothering to look up as Rosa finally peered around.

'Signor Luca, he *telefono* while you out. He will be back tonight.'

'Thank you, Rosa.'

The elderly lady turned to go, but midway she changed her mind. Crossing the room, she nervously perched herself on the edge of the bed, one bony hand touching Felicity's in a surprising gesture of warmth.

'You were right this morning,' she started, as Felicity looked up sharply, eternally suspicious of the other woman. 'You need some time alone with him. Tonight you cook, and me, Rosa, will go out. Come.' She gave Felicity the benefit of a very rare smile. 'I will show you how.'

Considering the internal bombshell that had just been dropped, Felicity found a strange sense of calm as she worked with Rosa in the kitchen. Old Italian music played on Rosa's equally ancient radio, the wood stove was warm and womblike, and the two woman worked quietly together, Felicity listing intently as Rosa indoctrinated her into the finer points of Italian cuisine.

Real Italian cuisine, Felicity realised, not the plastic-wrapped bags of pasta and jars of spicy sauce she was used to, or the tiny bottle of smelly parmesan that stayed in her cupboard gathering dust. Instead, under Rosa's patient guidance, Felicity turned a mountain of potatoes into tiny balls of *gnocchi*, rubbing the little bundles in flour, each one a labour of love in itself. She chopped onions and mushrooms, whisked eggs and fried bacon, until all that would be needed that night was a two-minute whisk in the saucepan while the gnocchi rose to the top of boiling water. And she learnt at twenty-six years of age that *real* parmesan cheese didn't smell at all, biting into the sharp, tiny curls Rosa shaved off, and suddenly discovering another vice to add to her list, along with chocolate and ice cream.

'*Grazie*, Rosa.' Felicity smiled as Rosa pulled on her coat, calling to her husband in rapid Italian.

'You are a good student.' Rosa shrugged. 'I hope you both have a nice night.'

As she turned to go Felicity felt a surge of panic.

For weeks now she had wanted this, a night alone with Luca, but now it was finally here she balked at the final hurdle, terrified of his reaction to the news she had to tell him. She wanted to call Rosa back, wanted the relative safety of an audience, but deep down Felicity knew she needed to face this alone.

She was having a baby.

And tonight Luca was going to find out.

CHAPTER NINE

LUCA'S methods of transport had some advantages.

The low throb of rotors nearing gave Felicity time for a final check. Lighting the candles, she flicked the switch on the CD player, hoping that the fact Puccini's *La Bohème* was at the top of the pile meant it was one of Luca's favourites. Standing at the fireplace, she checked her reflection for maybe the hundredth time.

A warm bath and the crackling fire she had lit brought a warmth to her pale cheeks that was so unfamiliar these days. Her blonde hair gleamed, piled high on her head and twisted into a coil, tendrils escaping around her face and neck, and a flash of lipstick accentuated her curvy mouth. The pale pink cashmere dress, another of her fabulous purchases, scooped low, her creamy décolletage for once filled something, and the soft pink hugged her swollen breasts, tapering into her waist. As the flash of helicopter lights flooded the lounge room she caught the reflection of her own glittering golden eyes. The nausea, so ever-present these days, was pleasantly absent—just the military march of her heart thumped as she struggled with her news.

Tried to fathom Luca's response.

'Where's Rosa?'

It wasn't exactly the most romantic of greetings, but given the frostiness of the morning's departure Felicity couldn't blame Luca. Barely dusting her cheeks with his lips he marched through the hallway and she clipped behind him in her heels. If anything his restless, brooding mood only made him more desirable, made it more imperative that she tell him the truth.

'I gave her the night off,' Felicity said in a falsely cheerful voice as Luca tossed his jacket in the vague direction of the couch. 'I thought it would be nice to spend some time together.'

'That wasn't the impression you gave this morning.' The sarcastic edge to his voice didn't go unnoticed. 'In fact this morning you gave the impression that some time *alone* was exactly what you wanted.'

Despite his aloofness Felicity knew he was hurt, knew that he was confused. After all, since their arrival in Italy she had hardly been the loving, giving wife he had so recently married. Constant nausea had put paid to that, but soon it would all be behind them. Once Luca understood the reason behind her distance they could finally move on, alone or together.

Now all she had to do was tell him.

'I did need some time alone this morning,' Felicity admitted slowly, bracing herself—but it was too soon; she wanted them to be sitting down, a meal between them, not this hostile confrontation. 'But now—'

'Oh, you've changed you mind,' Luca broke in, and Felicity snapped her mouth closed. 'Just like that.' He clicked his fingers so loudly, so close she jumped back. 'Never mind that I wanted to talk at the hotel. Never mind that you've pushed me away in bed for a full week. Now you've decided you want some quality time! Does it not enter your head that I might have had a bad day? That the very last thing I need right now is an in-depth discussion? That all I want to do is come home and have dinner?'

'I can understand you're upset, and I know it seems as if I've been pushing you away…' Felicity ventured as Luca pulled off his tie and simultaneously filled a whisky glass.

'You understand, do you?' Gulping his drink, he tore at his tie, cursing himself for his weakness. For weeks now she had pushed him away, the mere touch of him making her recoil. This morning's exchange had churned his stomach all day, and he wanted to hold that thought, to stay angry, to let her feel some of the pain he had, but he hadn't reckoned on this. Hadn't even contemplated coming home to her so sweet and warm, the effort she had gone to, the genuine appeal in her eyes—and that dress!

That body, wrapped, bathed in the softest pink, her breasts jutting out, her nipples swelling like berries… The need to touch, to possess was so strong he wanted to grab at those pins that held her hair, to feel it spill through his fingers, but more appealing, more utterly endearing, was seeing the fire in her eyes. The feisty woman he had first met seemed back now, the lethargic, tearful stranger had happily disappeared, but he couldn't let it go—couldn't just walk in and carry on as if nothing had happened, jump to her tune. There was too much pride and too much pain.

'I've cooked.'

'Why?' he asked rudely. 'I didn't bring you to the other side of the world to cook for me. Rosa is the cook; I employ her to cook for me.' An angry hand tossed at the air and Felicity felt her goodwill evaporate. Gorgeous he might be, but she damned well wasn't going to just stand there and let him walk over her…

'Oh, and I suppose a wife has other duties?' Felicity bit back.

'Exactly.' Downing his drink in one gulp, he turned

his fiery eyes to hers. 'So now I have a housekeeper who doesn't cook and a wife who doesn't like sex!'

His words were like a slap, but instead of defusing her mounting anger they only fired it. 'Well, maybe you should take more care with who you employ, Mr. Santanno,' Felicity retorted, her angry eyes a match for his, her chin jutting defiantly, five-foot-three of bristling indignation rising on her high heels. 'So far you don't appear to have a very good track record.'

'I assume by that you're referring to Matthew?' His voice was like ice, a muscle pounded in his cheek, and Felicity knew their argument had overstepped the mark, gone into uncharted territory. The festering boil needed to be lanced, but not like this; never like this. 'Do you really think he would have put up with this? His wife mooching around the house, barely talking, pretending to be asleep in bed at night?' He saw the colour rise on her cheek and gave a malevolent smile. 'You think I don't know when you pretend?'

'At least I knew where I stood with him!' Even as the words came out Felicity regretted them. There was no comparison in her relationships to Matthew and Luca. He was livid now, his olive skin tinged with grey, his eyes glinting dangerously as they narrowed, his hand so tight around the glass Felicity half expected it to shatter.

'Do I have to remind you that excuse of a man not only drugged you, he was blackmailing you also?' He slammed the glass down, and Felicity flinched as the verbal attack continued. 'I have never treated you with anything other than respect. Have I forced myself upon you? Have I pushed when it was clear you didn't want to sleep with me?' And you have the—the…' his fingers were snapping furiously, his mouth contorting in furious rage as he tried to fashion the word '...you have the—'

'Audacity, I think is the word you're looking for, Luca,' Felicity shouted, anger blurring her senses, crossing the invisible line they had drawn, pushing for a confrontation she wasn't sure she really wanted. But she was too fired up to care now. Tonight should have been so perfect. Tonight she had been going to tell him. And instead they were nose to nose, pouring out insults that could never be taken back. 'Yes, Luca, I have the audacity to expect my husband to understand that maybe I don't feel well, maybe there is a reason I'm not swinging off the chandeliers at the moment, and respect that, not rush off to another women's bed!'

He closed his eyes, every muscle in his face rigid as he raked his fingers through his hair. Dark, angry eyes finally opened, and for the briefest second the flash of pain she read in them cut her to the core. But the words that followed were more damning, more agonising than Felicity could ever have imagined.

'At least I know she wants me.'

How long they stood in stunned silence, Felicity didn't know. The spitting fire, the ticking clock, the low music were no match for the pounding in her temples, the vile taste of bile in her throat as she digested his words.

'Felice.' His voice came out in a low, weary moan, his head shaking as he tried to touch her, one hand reaching for her arm, but she shrugged it off, her face utterly white as she tried to fathom what he had just said. 'I shouldn't have said that.'

'Why not.' Her voice was a croak, her throat felt as if it had been sanded, and despite the heat of the fire, her raging pulse, she had never felt so icy-cold. 'It's hardly a State secret.'

'I should never have said it,' he said again, 'because it simply isn't true.'

'Isn't it?' Tears were now coursing, unchecked down her pale cheeks, but her voice was angry and strained. 'I'm sorry if I'm not very good at this—sorry if I'm not one of the sophisticated lovers you're used to. I don't know the rules, Luca, because I've never played before. I don't know what's real and what's imagined; I don't know how I'm supposed to react when half the village assumes that you're sleeping with Anna. And if your words were meant to give me some sort of cruel bedroom kick, then they worked, because you've hurt me.' A pale, trembling hand thumped at her chest, the fury lighting in her eyes again. 'You've hurt me and you promised you never would!'

A mass of flesh bore down on her, crushing her face with his kiss, quieting her protests, her doubts, her fury, her fears with the weight of his adoration. Hungry hands ravished her body, possessing it. Lowering her to the floor, he pulled at the dress. The tiny row of buttons at the back were too much to take in, the need to be inside her overwhelming both of them, and he pushed the soft fabric up over her thighs, ripping the tiny lace panties and tossing them aside, revelling in the sweet taste of her. She gasped beneath him, shocked and unsure at first, unable to believe he could be enjoying this, but his groans of approval were the confirmation she needed.

His closed eyes and rapt concentration allowed her a brief interlude to take in the feeling of him there, his probing tongue flicking at her swollen bud, her thighs tightening in spasms as her stomach tensed not with nerves, not with embarrassment or shame, but with the delicious trembling of her orgasm, deep, rapid contractions, that made her back arch. His strong hands held the peach of her trembling buttocks as she quivered under the mastery of his touch, tiny gasping sobs coming out of her parted lips, her body a delicious ball of tension, down to her curling toenails.

He had to stop, had to let her catch her breath, had to let the world stop spinning for a moment—only just as she thought it was over, just as he knelt back on his heels and the flickering pulse of her womanhood abated slightly, he pulled her dress higher, the sight of her engorged pink breasts meriting a slow kiss as he pulled down his zipper, as she moaned beneath him, exhausted, sure she had left that magical place he had taken her to, sure it was over for now.

The sight of him so swollen and virile stirred something in her almost akin to fear, her eyes widening with a thrill of sexual terror as he slowly parted her legs, dragging her along the cool tiles, every movement measured now, his eyes locking on hers, his voice a distant drum in the swirling fog of passion.

And he revelled in it, revelled in her innocence, in the feel of her gasping for him and him alone, adored the sound of strangled gasps that filled the vast room, the satin of her skin beneath his touch. He wanted so much to hold this moment for ever, to bathe in the beauty of her gaze, to treasure the feel of her, swollen and ready and welcome at his engorged tip, but he couldn't. The need to be inside her, to feel her wrapped around him, to plant his seed high in her womanhood was utterly overwhelming now, and he plunged inside her, simultaneously exploding as she gripped like a velvet vice.

'Felice.' His single word was more a moan, a gasp, as lay beside her, pulling her into the crook of his arm, his fingers making idle circles along her arms. The tiny, almost invisible hairs shivered as her nerves twitched, her body slowly winding down, ever down, and the world came back into focus. It took a moment to register that the phone was ringing, and they lay there for a silent moment, refusing to let a stranger intrude, relaxing when it stopped, when only the crackling fire and the sound of their breathing filled the room.

Now.

Closing her eyes, she took in a heady breath of the musky, citrus tang of his aftershave, the solid chest beneath her cheek, and for a moment in time she felt safe, sure that their lovemaking, the deeper union they had forged tonight, would sustain this onslaught.

'Luca…' Her voice was barely a whisper, her eyes still screwed closed as the dice started to roll, but the phone was ringing again, and Felicity froze in his arms as he cursed at the intrusion.

'It might be important,' he said, reluctantly untangling himself, quickly sorting his clothes. She fumbled on the floor, pulling down her dress as he picked up the phone. *'Pronto?'*

As Luca's voice became more urgent, her forehead creased. He spoke loudly, but she tried to convince herself that nothing was wrong. Italians always shouted into the telephone, she'd learnt, always sounded as if World War III had broken out or the family was about to be ripped to shreds by marauding wolves, when all they were discussing was the weather.

'It's Ricardo.' As Luca replaced the receiver the reassuring smile didn't come, his face paling as he walked over. 'He has had a heart attack.'

'Oh, my God.' Sinking to the couch, Felicity shook her head. 'I saw Anna just this morning. She said he had chest pain, but they thought it was just indigestion.'

'It was his heart. They've taken him to a hospital in Rome, the best, but he nearly died on the way. They managed to revive him, but he is very sick. Anna is very upset.'

A smart retort that was absolutely out of place bobbed on Felicity's tongue, but she bit it back. Ricardo was a close friend of Luca; the last thing he needed was a sarcastic comment from his wife. Still, Felicity wasn't quite convinced Anna really was that upset. Her dismissive words about her husband this morning still reeled in Felicity's mind. If she'd called a doctor, taken him to the hospital then, instead of buying indigestion liquid, surely this could have been avoided, surely…

'I have to go.'

'To Anna?' Felicity gasped, unable to comprehend what he was saying and praying she'd somehow misheard.

'She's upset; she's alone at the *infermeria*. I couldn't say no to her. Come with me.'

Instantly she shook her head. The word *infirmeria* had sent an icy chill through her spine, memories of Joseph's death too utterly painful even to tentatively explore. 'I can't.'

'Can't or won't?' His words were sneering, but seeing the pain in her eyes he stopped, one hand tentatively catching her cheek.

'That's where Joseph died.'

'Oh, Felice.' His words were gentler now, her palpable pain reaching him. 'I am so sorry for your pain. But you of all people must realise how Anna is feeling;

surely you can understand why she needs me to go to her?'

But Felicity *didn't* understand; the part of helpless female was one she had never played before. Her mind whizzed back a year, to here in this very city, sitting on a hard-backed chair as Joseph neared his painful end, her parents, exhausted from their mercy flight, grabbing a few hours' sleep back at the hotel.

My God, she didn't even speak the language, but it had never even entered her head to wake her father in the middle of the night, to call him to fetch her. Why the hell couldn't Anna get a taxi? 'Surely she's got family, friends? Why does it have to be you?'

'Because it's always me!' Luca's words were sharp—bitter, even. 'Anything happens in this village, it is me they call.' His voice softened then, and taking both her hands, he looked at her, imploring her to understand. 'If it was you alone at the hospital Ricardo would do the same. I wouldn't expect any less from him, and I cannot let him down.'

'But you can let *me* down?' She could hear the jealous edge to her voice, see the weary resignation in his eyes as he shook his head, but still she couldn't stop herself. Tonight meant everything; tonight there was so much she wanted—no, needed to say. But Anna clicked her fingers and Luca ran. 'We've just made love, Luca. There are things I need to talk about.'

'Me, me me!' He shook his head, his eyes blazing. 'You know, I almost feel sorry for you! You're like a jealous two-year-old. Again and again I tell you it is over. It has been for years between Anna and me...'

'She tried to make love to you the other week,' Felicity retorted, but still Luca wouldn't relent.

'She made a mistake! She knows it is all over between us. I am married to you and Anna respects that! Has she not tried to be friends with you? Has she not rung you several times and tried to go for coffee? You moan you are lonely, that there is no one to talk to, yet when someone extends the hand of friendship you pull away.'

'She used to be your lover!' She was shouting now, utterly perplexed that he couldn't see her point of view. 'How can I be friends with someone you slept with? Mind you, maybe I'd better get used to it—after all, if you lined up all your ex-lovers half the female population would be ruled out.' Bitching was something Felicity wasn't used to, something she'd never done, but then again she'd never been in love before, never ridden the rollercoaster of emotions that came when you gave away your heart to a lousy playboy. The words that tumbled from her lips, and the scoffing laugh that followed were so alien Felicity almost didn't recognise her own voice.

His finger razored her cheek, his head shaking with almost weary resignation. 'You know, I thought you were so gentle, so sweet—that underneath that harsh exterior there was a warm loving woman inside. I guess even I get things wrong sometimes.'

She watched him go, and her heart didn't feel as if it was beating any more. She watched his car snake down the mountainside with dry eyes that couldn't even expend a tear.

Had she really got things so wrong?

Looking around, she saw the telltale remnants of their passionate encounter, the candle wicks spitting in the puddles of wax. She blew them out with pale lips, picking up her discarded shoes and underpants and making her way up the stairs to the vast lonely bed.

She tried and failed not to imagine Anna in Luca's arms, that beautiful, calculating raven head resting on his chest, tried to believe the comfort Luca imparted to her would be as innocent as he swore.

The cotton sheets were cool on her body, and her hand moved down to the hollow of her stomach, resting naturally on the tiny life within.

Luca's child.

She lay there for an age, staring at the ceiling. The heavy snow of the mountains muffled sound, creating an eerie silence, paving the way for her own self-doubts to voice themselves loudly. The moon drifting past gobbled up minutes, turning them into hours as she waited for the master to return, waited for Anna to have her fill.

And finally, when dawn was breaking, when a million taunting questions had made a mockery of each and every platitude she'd attempted to deliver, it was with hurt, jealous eyes that she turned to Luca as he crept into the bedroom, the cool night air following him in, sending a shiver across the bed as he pulled off his coat.

'How is he?'

'No change.' Luca shrugged. 'I only got to see him for a moment; the doctor said he should rest.'

'But…'

She sat up, confused eyes locking on his. Never had he looked more beautiful. The early-morning five o'clock shadow darkened his chin, accentuating the razor-sharp lines of his cheekbones, his black hair was laced with snowflakes, and she ached, physically ached to put her hand up, to let her fingers massage, capture that face in the palm of her hand, to pull that cold tired body into the warm bed, to kiss away the stern taut flexion of his lips. But, as beautiful as he might look, never had he seemed more unobtainable.

Trying and failing to keep her voice even, to eloquently put forward her point without lacing each word with the bitter sound of jealousy, she spoke again. 'You've been gone six hours.'

'Anna was upset.' His eyes locked on hers, defiant, angry eyes, without a hint of contrition.

'And naturally you had to comfort her,' Felicity sneered.

Tonight should have been so special. Tonight should have been about babies and plans and moving forward. Instead Anna had yet again impinged on them. Anna's shadow had again darkened the door of their relationship. Frankly, Felicity was sick of it.

'Actually—' his eyes were like ice, his words laced with scorn, '—as it turned out, Anna ended up comforting me. Ricardo has been like a father to me since my own died. Seeing him lying there, so old and so feeble all of a sudden, hit me in a way I didn't expect and Anna understood. I never really expected my wife to.'

CHAPTER TEN

'YOU'VE both been wonderful.'

Anna's deep, throbbing voice still set Felicity's teeth on edge, but, bracing herself, she poured Anna's third *limoncello* into a glass and offered it to the pale woman sitting on the sofa, her raven hair cascading down her shoulders, her unbuttoned coat slipping enough to show a mocking curve of voluptuous creamy bosom.

To say she had seen more of Anna than Luca in the last few days since Ricardo's heart attack would be the understatement of the millennium. Anna would appear in the kitchen, draped in cashmere or fur, as Felicity struggled to focus, then disappeared with Luca in a waft of nauseating perfume, only to return at some ungodly hour and regale Felicity with snippets of Ricardo's progress while Luca disappeared into the study to make a few international calls, surfacing to drive his ex-mistress the short journey home.

Their marriage, if you could call it that, had eclipsed the rowing stage, bypassed the acrimonious one, and seemed to have slipped into the rather more terminal state of weary resignedness.

'Where's Rosa?' Anna asked, taking a hefty sip of her drink.

'Felice gave her the night off. Again,' Luca added, with a hint of an edge to his voice that Anna instantly picked up on.

'She wants her husband to herself, darling,' she drawled. 'And frankly I don't blame her.' Felicity was just about to come up with a withering reply, but her response faded on her lips as Anna continued. 'She really is a most difficult woman. I don't know why you still employ her, Luca.'

'But you get on with her,' Felicity pointed out.

'Only because I'm out of her precious Luca's life. She treated me like dirt on a shoe when I was here, but now that I am gone she has exalted me to saint-like status. I don't blame you for wanting rid of her and to have the house to yourself. I know that when I get Ricardo home I am going to do everything for him. The hospital has organised nurses to come to the house but I don't want them. I am going to take care of him myself. This has been a big…'

'Wake-up call?' Felicity's voice was barely a croak as she finished Anna's sentence.

'That's what I am trying to say.' Anna smiled gratefully. 'Seeing him so ill, so frail and being able to do nothing.' She closed her eyes and a tear slid down her cheek. 'That night when I called, I am sorry I disturbed you, but the nurse was saying I had to go home, to find his medication and bring it back, to get some rest. My tears were upsetting Ricardo. I shouldn't have disturbed you… '

'Nonsense.' Sitting beside Anna on the couch, Felicity took the other woman's cold hand and gave it a small squeeze, offering her first genuine response to Anna. 'Of course you should have rung; we're friends.'

Looking up, she saw the start in Luca's expression, registered the tiny grateful smile he gave her, and the guilt that had been niggling at her for the past week suddenly multiplied.

Anna wasn't just upset; she was genuinely distraught. The brash, man-eating vixen Felicity had imagined seemed far removed from the pale, wan woman sitting trembling on the sofa.

'I'd better go.' Standing, she buttoned her coat, gesturing for Luca to sit down as he rummaged for his car keys. 'I can walk. It is only a few minutes, and the fresh air will do me good.'

'You mustn't walk.' It was Felicity who was insisting now, Felicity, handing Luca his keys. 'It's been snowing again; Luca will drive you.'

Standing in the lounge, she wiped the fog from the steamed-up window, watching as Luca opened the passenger door, gently guiding Anna into the seat. His hand on the small of her back was a simple action that only a few moments ago would have spun her into a frenzy of jealousy, but Anna's grief had touched her.

When Luca returned he was tired, pale and tense.

'Was I too long for you?' he snapped as he walked in, tossing his coat over the pale sofa and kicking off his shoes. 'Did you expect me to just drop her off at the gates?'

'Of course not.'

'She offered me a coffee,' Luca volunteered, unmoved by her response. 'But naturally I declined. I wouldn't want to give you more ammunition.'

'Luca, please, I don't want to fight.'

'Neither do I.' Suddenly all the fight seemed to go out of him. Lines she had never seen before were grooved beside his eyes, and Felicity realised there and then how much the last few days had taken their toll. The last few weeks, come to that.

Horrified by what had happened at the golf resort, Luca had been springing surprise visits on every hotel he owned, calling meetings, leaving at the crack of dawn and not returning until late at night in an effort to ensure no one else would suffer the way her family had.

And what had she done in return?

Moaned she was lonely, carried on like a spoilt two-year-old, devoid of attention.

And now his dear friend was sick, and he was stuck with a jealous wife, questioning his every move.

Well, no more.

'I don't want to fight either. Luca, I'm sorry for doubting you. Seeing Anna tonight has made me realise how selfish I've been—not just to her, but to you as well. It can't have been easy for you these past few weeks.' Swallowing hard, she tried to plan her words, but nothing came. What was more disturbing was the noticeable absence of Luca's response to her attempt at an apology. 'Luca, what I'm trying to say is—'

'Save it.' He didn't snap, there wasn't even a trace of malice in his voice, but right now Felicity would have preferred it. Their passionate rows, volatile encounters left her spinning and reeling, but this lethargic response to her heartfelt apology was far more worrying, and her eyes widened with anxiety as Luca shrugged her hand off his arm and headed for the stairs.

'Luca, please.'

He turned briefly, his face so jaded, so utterly, utterly exhausted it momentarily stopped Felicity in her tracks.

'I'm tired, Felice. I've been getting up at five every morning, not getting home till after midnight. Surely you can understand that even I need to sleep occasionally?'

'It's not Anna that I want to speak about, Luca,' Felicity implored. 'It's us.'

A tight smile twitched his grim lips. 'I'm sure the row will keep till morning.'

The abyss between them as she lay in the massive bed seemed to stretch for ever. She mentally willed Luca to roll over, to reach for her in his sleep as he always had…

Till now.

A tentative hand reached for one broad shoulder. Even in sleep she could feel his tension, feel the taut muscles under her hands. A tiny shrug as he subconsciously dismissed her had her hand pulling back as if she had touched hot coal, and an awful sense of foreboding filled her, her stomach spasming simultaneously with her heart as Luca rolled further to his edge of the bed and further out of her life.

He awoke at the first ring of his alarm, jumping out of bed with military control when surely his body must be aching for a few more hours of undisturbed rest, and she watched him through sleep-deprived eyes. Her whole night had been spent tossing and turning, and the pain in her stomach was one she didn't want to acknowledge, but one she couldn't ignore.

'You look terrible.' He was knotting his tie, fresh-shaven now, utterly in control.

Utterly out of reach.

'I didn't get much sleep,' Felicity admitted, pulling her knees up to her stomach and wishing the pain would abate, wishing he would just go so she could deal with whatever her body was dishing out. Privacy was something she craved now.

'Maybe this will make you feel better.' Reaching into his briefcase, he handed her a bundle of papers, watching with questioning eyes as Felicity struggled to sit up, noting her flushed cheeks as she slowly turned the mountain of pages. 'It is the deeds for the golf resort. You will see your father is the owner now.' A tiny pause, a tiny hesitation—and, though Felicity couldn't be sure, a tiny tinge of sadness before he carried on talking. 'It is watertight, Felice. My lawyers have been working on it all week; I cannot suddenly change my mind.'

Tears pricked her eyes as she felt the mattress indent, watched one large, dark-skinned hand move across the sheet and take hers.

'We haven't made each other very happy, have we? I'm tired of fighting, and seeing you so sad, like a prisoner here—well, it isn't what I intended.' His hand tightened around hers, and Felicity had to bite through her bottom lip to stop herself from crying out as Luca went on. 'You've got what you wanted. Matthew's out of your life and your father has his resort back, which is no less than he deserves.'

'But what about you?' Her voice was a mere croak as cruel reality hit.

'Me?' He gave a low laugh. 'With your permission, of course, I'll tell my mother that my one attempt at marriage has put me off for life. It should keep her off my back for a couple of years at least—so, you see, it hasn't been a total waste of time.'

It was over, over, over, and if anything Luca was relieved.

'What I said about Anna...' Felicity started, but Luca just shook his head.

'It isn't just about Anna, Felice; you know that deep down. It is as much my fault. You wanted details and I refused to give them, but I didn't think I should have to spell everything out.'

Bemused, she stole a look from under tear-laden eyelashes, her lips parting, longing to stop him, to halt the horrible end, but Luca carried on relentlessly, his farewell speech obviously well rehearsed—no questions from the back of the room, please!

'I didn't just want *fun*, a mistress with a ring on her finger. I wanted a wife.'

'I want to be your wife,' Felicity begged, but Luca just shook his head.

'Ricardo is like my second father—you know that, I have told you again and again, but have you come to the hospital with me? Have you held my hand, been there for me? I know that the hospital has bad memories for you, I know about Joseph, and I would have supported you through that, been there to help you if only you had met me halfway. Shown me you cared.'

'I do care,' Felicity insisted, but it fell on deaf ears.

'Anna is not my lover, not my mistress. Over and over I have told you, yet you steadfastly refuse to believe me. Felice I cannot live like this, cannot face the accusation in your eyes every time I am home ten minutes late. I explained on my first day with you how things were; I thought you would trust me. I admit I have said some hurtful things, but that was in the heat of a row—a row you continually instigated.' He let his words sink in for a moment before continuing, more gently this time. 'You are holding back from me. Every day I feel I know you a bit less; every day I feel you distance yourself a bit more.'

Standing, he stared at her for an age, before depositing a soft kiss on her cheek and heading for the door.

'We both deserve better, Felice; you know that as well as I do.'

Watching him leave, watching him turn and walk away, was like seeing the coffin lowered. She wanted to fling herself on him, to beg for a second chance, for the hands of time to pull back, for the powers that be to breathe life into all she had lost. But, battling with nausea and grief, all she could do was stumble from the bed. The heavy door closed and the tears finally came, the pain in her stomach a dull ache compared to the loss in her heart.

She had lost him, lost the only man she had ever loved, and her nausea trebled. Hearing the chopper thudding overhead, pulling him away with every swoop of its rotors, she was literally overwhelmed by grief. Beads of sweat rose on her brow, and the pain in her stomach ripped through her like a gunshot. Felicity felt as if her world had been ripped apart at the seams.

She only just made it to the bathroom in time.

CHAPTER ELEVEN

SOMETHING was wrong.

Rinsing her mouth at the sink, Felicity caught sight of her ashen face in the mirror. Only two spots of color flamed, but her skin felt as if it were on fire. Resting her cheek against the cool mirror, she closed her eyes, begging the room to stop spinning, for her breathing to even out, for the pain in her stomach to abate somewhat.

She couldn't be losing the baby. Felicity battled with a tidal wave of emotions. The little life she had felt so equivocal about suddenly took on momentous proportions. Telling Luca she loved him would be so much easier without a baby on board, so less complicated without a pregnancy to comprehend, but Mother Nature was playing her cards now, signing Felicity up for a crash course in maternal instinct, and she sank to the floor, hugging her knees to her chest, trying to somehow protect the tiny life within as gradually, mercifully, the pain lessened.

With or without Luca, this baby was everything to her.

It wasn't just a Santanno, it was her child, and losing it now would be like losing her soul.

'*Signora!*' Rosa was tapping on the door, her voice annoyingly loud, and Felicity struggled into a robe and pulled open the bedroom door. 'Signor Santanno just telephone—he forget his briefcase. He needs some papers for a lunchtime meeting, so my husband is going to drive it to Rome for him and drop it into Reception.'

'Okay.' Her voice sounded amazingly normal as she retrieved the case from the floor.

'Signora Felicity!' Rosa did a double-take as she took the case and made to go. 'You look terrible.'

'So everyone keeps telling me,' Felicity said dryly, then forced a smile. 'I'm fine, Rosa; I've got a stomach upset, that's all.' She was about to blame it on something she'd eaten, but, anticipating the hysterics that would send the elderly woman into, Felicity quickly changed tack. 'A bit of gastric flu or something.'

'Do you want me to send for the doctor?'

Felicity hesitated. A doctor was exactly what she needed, but not with Rosa hovering anxiously downstairs. Luca deserved to hear the news from her first.

'Rosa, could you ask Marco to wait? I'll only be five minutes. I want to go into Rome myself; if he wouldn't mind giving me a lift that would be great.'

'But you are sick.'

Oh, she was sick, Felicity thought sadly. Sick of the lies, sick of putting everything off, sick of avoiding confrontation.

'I need to see my husband,' Felicity said firmly, and Rosa gave a heavy shrug. 'I'll get dressed now.'

The journey seemed to take for ever. Battling with nausea, forcing a smile as the questioning eyes of Marco surveyed her from the rearview mirror. All she knew was that she had to see Luca, tell him the truth and then take it from there. Together they would go to the hospital. Together they would face the truth about their unborn child.

Gradually the lush mountains gave way to the occasional village, soon joining into one mass of streets, and the coiling, writhing city came to life before her eyes as they battled the heavy traffic. The inevitable horns, the beautiful women and handsome men rushing along the streets, the pavement cafés littered with lovers and smart businessmen, backpackers and tourists, all descending on this most beautiful city.

Just as she had left it a year ago.

A sign for the Trevi Fountain came into view as the car slowed, and for a moment so did Felicity's heart.

'One coin means you'll come back, two to marry an Italian, three to live happily ever after.' Joseph's voice echoed through her mind. The last precious days of Joseph's life, those poignant final days, days that had been too painful for recollection until now.

God, she missed him so.

'Ére.' Marco's voice snapped her mind to attention as they drew up outside the hotel, the door opening before the car had even come to a halt, and as the green-uniformed man realised who she was he called for the concierge, Rafaello.

'*Bongiorno*, Signora Felicity,' Rafaello called as he flew down the steps to greet her, a beaming smile splitting his face as he tried to relieve her of the briefcase. 'This is a pleasant surprise! Allow me to take Signor Santanno's case for you; I will take it to him directly.'

'*Bongiorno*, Rafaello.' Felicity returned the warm greeting as he walked towards the revolving doors. 'But there's really no need. I'll take it to Luca myself.'

'It is no problem, *signora*.' Suddenly the beaming smile didn't seem quite so natural, and Felicity felt her eyes narrow as her fingers tightened around the handle. 'I will arrange some morning tea for you. Signor Santanno is in a meeting.'

They were crossing the courtyard now, and Felicity

felt every last vestige of hope, of trust disappear as Rafaello carried on talking, the beautiful, lyrical accent grating now as the ream of excuses pounded in her ears.

'I will let him know you are here, and no doubt he will come down directly, but he made it very clear he didn't want to be disturbed.'

'Did he, now?' Felicity's voice was quiet, but strong. She had come here to face the truth, but it would seem from the staff's reaction that the truth might be a touch more complicated than she had envisaged.

Her eyes met Rafaello's head-on. 'I don't want morning tea—thank you for asking. And I most certainly don't want to sit and wait. My husband wants his case, and I intend to take it up to him.'

'But *signora*...'

'Please.' Putting up a slightly trembling hand, Felicity stopped Rafaello mid-flow. Whatever life was about to throw at her, it needed to be faced. She was tired of following Luca's golden path, tired of the staff that smoothed over the cracks, tired of Luca's refusal to follow life's simple moral code. 'This isn't your problem.'

Cheeks burning, she strode through the golden revolving doors, barely acknowledging the grandeur of her surroundings as she spun through the massive foyer, ignoring the agonised looks from the concierge as he gestured to one of his staff to pick up the telephone. It was an old-fashioned lift, and as the gates pulled closed she felt as if she were being imprisoned, locked in her own eternal hell. She braced herself for what was to come as she rummaged in her purse for her swipe card.

Poor Rafaello would be joining Ricardo in the coronary care unit, Felicity thought ruefully as he burst through the stairwell door, admitting defeat with a sorry shrug as she determinedly swiped her card and pushed open the heavy door.

She'd thought she had prepared herself for the sight that might greet her, but the pain that seared through her as she took in the scene told Felicity that nothing ever truly prepared a person for loss.

Anticipation was no antidote for confirmation.

'Felice!'

She couldn't look at him, couldn't bring herself to face the man who had just broken her heart. Instead her eyes worked the room, taking in the massive floral bouquets, the champagne cooling in a silver bucket, the candles burning, *La Bohème* throbbing through the heavy air, and finally she dragged her eyes to where Luca stood, Anna just a foot away, her raven curls still falling from being hastily pushed away by him—but not hastily enough.

The image of her in his arms, of that beautiful face resting on that strong chest in this most beautiful of surroundings was etched on Felicity's mind for ever.

'Ho provato a telefonare, il signore.'

The Italian was rapid, but it didn't take Einstein to work out what Rafaello was saying, and with a strange surge of confidence Felicity watched their stunned faces as she managed a translation.

'Which might have helped—' Felicity gave a thin smile as she crossed the room to the bedside table '—if the telephone hadn't been taken off the hook. You were right, Rafaello; Signor Santanno really didn't want to be disturbed after all.'

'Felice, please.' Tossing Anna to one side, Luca was next to her in a second, grabbing at her arm, swinging her around and forcing her to face him. 'This is not how it seems. Tell her Anna.' His pleading eyes hardened as he turned to his smirking mistress. 'Tell her how you planned this, tell her I knew nothing about it…'

'Come now, Luca.' The smirk widened to a malicious grin as she sidled over, her rounded hips sashaying across the room, tossing her mane of hair, not a trace of contrition as she faced Felicity. And for a second, for a horrible moment, Felicity swore she saw pity in those beautiful almond eyes. 'Felicity had to find out about us sooner or later. I'm sure given time she'll come to understand.'

'Understand this!' Her words were like pistol-shots, the pity in Anna's eyes neither wanted nor needed. 'You can have him, Anna—all of him. And I didn't *just* find out; I've known all along. The only mistake I made was believing Luca when he told me how much he thought you'd changed, but I think his first assessment of you was rather more correct.'

'And what was that?' A flicker of doubt flashed in her eyes, and a muscle was pounding in her smooth olive cheek as she turned questioningly to Luca, but it was Felicity who answered her.

'Well, you'll have to forgive my rather poor Italian, and I'm sure you'll understand if my pronunciation isn't quite correct, but the word *puttana* is the one that springs to mind.' And, turning on her heel, she left the room, ignoring Luca's calls, even managing a hollow laugh at Anna's emerging hysterics.

He caught up with her at the lift, blocking the gap with his shoulder as she slammed the heavy iron gates. Even though it must have been agony, he barely winced as she struggled to close them. 'Felicity, you have it all wrong.'

'No, I don't,' she shouted. 'You told me she'd changed, told me you were taking her to the hospital every morning, told me she was sitting at her husband's bedside, willing him to live—and look what was really going on. God, I even insisted you drove her home last night; you must have been laughing yourselves sick in the car. Poor, blind Felicity. Poor, trusting Felicity. I trusted, you Luca; I trusted you and look where that got me.'

'You've never trusted me!' His voice was a roar, and the urgency in it, the sheer volume behind it startled her.

A surge of nervousness had her forcing the lift gate closed as she wrestled to keep him out. Like a keeper slamming the gate on a deranged animal. Only when the gate was firmly shut did she look at him again, but her hand was on the button, pushing for the ground floor as she prayed for the beastly lift to move.

'You never trusted me,' he shouted again, 'not for a single moment, but you have to trust me now.'

'Why? So you can humiliate me again? So you can carry on your sordid little affair with an air of respectability? Well, forget it, Luca. A mistress with a ring is something I'll never be.'

'Come out of this lift this instant.' His voice was still loud, still packed its usual authoritarian punch, but there was such raw urgency in it, such an air of desperation that Felicity almost did as he begged. But this bitter end was just too painful to face. The lift was starting to move, beginning its slow descent, and maybe it was for the best, she decided. What was the point in hearing more lies, shovelling hurt onto hurt?

But there was one more thing she needed to say, three little words that would prove the magnitude of her pain, so he clearly knew just what he had flicked away.

'I loved you, Luca—loved you all along. And just look where it got me!' Her words echoed upwards as she shouted to the walls.

Slamming at the gate, wrestling with the weight of iron, if he could have put his hand through the metal-work and grabbed the thick oily chain, somehow held onto her, Luca would have. Instead he gripped onto the gate, gripped for a second or two as her final words washed over him, screwing his eyes closed as the truth finally dawned.

That surly, moody chameleon who had shared his bed, who had teetered into his life on too-high heels in a too-tight dress, had really, truly loved him.

'Luca?' Anna was coming over, but he barely even recognised her, didn't even have it in him to be angry with her at this moment. Nothing seemed to matter now. Nothing except what he had lost. 'It is for the best. Felicity is too soft for you—too soft to be a Santanno. She will be okay.'

But as Luca turned, as Anna saw his broken, shattered face, heard that usually strong voice so hoarse, so bereft, for the first time in her life she felt an alien sting of guilt, a rumble of shame, and she watched the man she adored dissolve before her eyes.

'She probably will,' he mumbled, speaking in English, the only thread he had left that bound him to Felice. 'But will I?'

CHAPTER TWELVE

THROUGH the tiny steep backstreets she ran, slipping, stumbling, but not caring, immune to the curious looks of the locals as she ran sobbing by. There was no master plan, no direction or purpose to her journey, just an overwhelming need for space, for distance. Gulping air into her lungs, she felt the cool rain on her burning face and only then did she register where she was.

The Trevi Fountain. Neptune standing proud and tall, just as she had left him a year ago, water cascading, the glitter of coins at the bottom, tossed in the eternal hope that the world would keep on turning, that life would go on and that one day in the future you surely would return. But all Felicity felt as she stared into the water was agony, and wonder at how a city so beautiful could have caused so much pain, how she could be holding a place responsible for taking away so much that was dear.

Her brother.

Her husband.

And as her hands moved to her stomach, as the pain that had engulfed her through the night returned with a vengeance, Felicity knew the city had staked its final claim, that the baby she had only just begun to hold dear was surely about to be its final victim.

It was Joseph's voice ringing in her ears as she sank to the floor, Joseph's voice playing over and over as she registered the horror in the onlookers' eyes, heard in the distance their chaotic shouting, the distant wail of sirens drawing closer.

'I should ask for a refund.'

The paramedics didn't get it. Instead they mumbled about her being delirious as they loaded her into the ambulance.

Drifting in and out of consciousness she lay there still; nothing more could hurt her now. Even the overhead signs for *Emergenza* as they raced her through the stark tiled corridors of the hospital barely touched her. The oxygen mask smelt funny, and the drip maybe stung a bit, but such was her grief, such was her loss it didn't really matter.

Nothing mattered any more.

CHAPTER THIRTEEN

HE WAS beautiful.

It was the first thought that popped into Felicity's mind as her heavy eyes opened. She battled an overwhelming urge to close them again, to let the drug-induced oblivion descend on her once again.

He lay dozing in the chair beside her bed, but even sleep didn't seem to relax him. His weary features were ravaged with lines, the shadow dusting his chin as dark as night, as dark as the hollows smudged under his eyes. Looking down, she saw his dark hand clasped over hers, his fingers carefully avoiding the drip that seeped into her thin vein, the flash of his heavy gold watch.

The hospital tape over her wedding ring seemed fitting somehow.

Masking the union that should never have been.

He was as beautiful as he had been when she had first laid eyes on him, just a few short weeks ago, only now there was so much more between them than ships that passed in the night. A marriage in smithereens, an aching, gaping void where her heart had once been.

Yet she couldn't regret it.

Somewhere deep inside she still attempted to justify the pain that had been inflicted. The bliss she had found in his arms, the warmth that had bathed her when those mocking, calculating eyes had occasionally lowered their guard, when those strong arms had held her as a man should hold a woman, the childlike belief that Luca really could make everything all right.

'Felice?' His concerned face hovered over hers. His jacket had been discarded, and as her eyes flicked down she saw the savage smear of Anna's lipstick on his collar—an awful reminder of what had taken place if ever she'd needed one. Wincing, she tore her eyes away, and he misinterpreted her agony. 'Here—' Pushing a tiny cord into her hand, he wrapped her fingers over a switch. 'Push this. It takes away the pain.'

Nothing will take away my pain. She nearly said it, drugs and emotion were a dangerous cocktail, but somewhere within she still had pride, still had a piece of her left that Luca Santanno could never destroy. Instead of looking at him she turned her face to the bland curtains, worked her tired eyes around the room, its familiarity doing nothing to soothe her.

The rooms were undoubtedly all the same here, so why should she think that this was the same one where Joseph had died? That the beige curtains and rickety bedside table were exclusive to her loss?

Losses.

The baby bobbed into her consciousness then, the tiny scrap of life she had never really met, never consciously desired. But now it was gone Felicity realised with a piercing sense of loss just how desperately it had been wanted.

Her baby.

Tears squeezed out of her eyes, salty heavy tears, each one loaded with agony for the loss of a little life so precious. As Luca pressed the button deeper into her hand she resolutely pushed it away. Somehow she wanted, *needed* to feel the pain, needed the physical agony. Her body demanded this memorial to all she had lost.

'I'm sorry.'

How meaningless his words were, how utterly utterly, empty his apology when their child was dead.

'I should have listened to you.' Gently, so as not to hurt her further, he lowered himself onto the bed, the mattress indenting, the scent of him filling her. Yet still her face stayed turned away; still she couldn't bring herself to look at him. 'I couldn't understand why you didn't trust me, why you insisted that there was something between Anna and I.'

'You couldn't understand?' They were the first words she had spoken, and when they came her voice was hoarse with emotion. 'How can you say that when all the time you were lying to me? Was I supposed to just melt into a corner? To turn a blind eye when you slept with your mistress? Is that the language you understand?'

'Since Anna and I parted I have never slept with her.'

'Oh, save it, Luca.' Her hand was working the tiny button now, pushing the switch furiously, listening to the tiny bleeps that meant a cure was being delivered. But this was a pain no drug could deal with; this was an agony modern medicine would never cure. The cure for a broken heart was as elusive as the cure for the common cold, and the disease probably just as prevalent. 'I saw you; I caught you, don't try and deny it now. Your staff knew, Rafaello nearly had a coronary racing to warn you your little wife was on her way up, and yet you have the gall to sit here and tell me that you're not sleeping together.'

For the first time he didn't rise, didn't match her

fury. Instead he pulled the switch from her, then tightened his hand around her cold, trembling fingers. 'You need to be awake for this, Felice. You are going to listen to me and you are going to believe me. I have been naïve.'

To hear such a strong, assured man make this admission had her turning momentarily to him, her forehead puckering as he falteringly continued. 'Till I met you I had never been jealous in my life. It is an emotion I have never encountered, and then you came along.'

His hand tightened on hers, only this time it wasn't tenderly. 'When I thought about you and Matthew, when I imagined him making love to you, I felt this sick, churning loathing and I didn't even recognise it. Didn't understand that the emotion I was experiencing was jealousy. The same jealousy Anna was feeling. And, from my brief encounter with it, I am starting to understand how it can make you do strange things.

'That first day when you were in my room, demanding your dress, heading back to him, all I knew was that I had to stop you. I would have done anything to stop you, *anything*, and that is what Anna was doing. In her mind she believed if she told everyone we were still together, if enough people—you included—thought it was happening, then perhaps it really would. She engineered things right down to the last detail. She drove enough of a wedge between us to ensure that doubt was there, and then stepped in like a vulture swooping on her prey. But I would never have slept with her. *Never.*

'Walking into the hotel room, I was furious. I finally realised how right you had been to be suspicious, just how calculating Anna had been all along. I told her to get out; she just refused to accept it, kept on throwing herself on me, begging me to reconsider. That was when you walked in.'

Oh, she wanted to believe him, wanted to so badly it hurt, but she was too raw, too scared to just accept his story, to believe it could all be so straightforward.

'I should hate Anna, but I don't,' Luca said more softly. 'I pity her—and, more pointedly, I can understand her motives. Understand how jealousy can make you do the strangest things. How it can strike at the strangest times. How it can toss aside reason and make you act on impulse.'

'Like asking a stranger to marry you?' Felicity ventured, and Luca gave a tired nod.

'In my mind I really believed that if I married you, loved you, told the world you were my wife, somehow one day you might end up loving me back. I love you Felice.'

'No false declarations, remember?' Pulling her hand away, she stared at the bland wall. His pity was the one thing she couldn't take. But Luca's hands were cupping her face, turning her to face him.

'How can it be a false declaration when I am speaking from my heart? I love you. I have done from the second you fell into my arms, from the moment I held you and you wept. When you called out in your sleep and I came to lie beside you, I knew there and then that I never wanted to let you go again. I barely knew you and yet I would have done anything to keep you. You were right. I did sabotage your plans to study, did put off talking to the lawyer—but only because I couldn't bear the thought of losing you. Couldn't stand to see you walking out of my life before we'd even started.'

She lay there, his words washing over her, utterly

floored as he carried on in that delicious faltering voice. This strong, beautiful man was telling her the one thing she needed to hear.

Luca Santanno loved her.

And it should have helped; only it didn't. The omission of any declaration of love in their relationship had cost the life of their child.

The hope that had briefly invaded her war torn body dispersed then. Lying back on the starched white pillow, she closed her eyes, retrieving her hand from his grasp.

Love seemed small compensation for such an overwhelming loss.

'You knew about the baby, didn't you?' His voice was soft, thick, and laced with uncertainty. Slowly she nodded, the tears sliding down her cheeks into her hair. 'That is why you were so sick, why you were so—so…'

'Difficult?' Felicity finished for him. 'I've never been so scared in my life, never felt so sick, and I just didn't know what to do—how to tell you.'

'I wish you had,' he said, but with not a hint of reproach in his voice. 'Surely I'm not that unapproachable?'

'You are.' Felicity sighed. 'But not enough to keep me from loving you. And you made it very clear from the start that you didn't want babies.'

'I *didn't* want babies,' Luca agreed. 'Frankly, I couldn't see what all the fuss was about. I'd watched friends and family turn from competent professionals to neurotic parents, discussing unmentionable things at the dinner table, debating for hours the merits of breastfeeding versus bottles, then you came along and suddenly there I was wondering if we'd have blonde or dark-haired children, children with your reserve or my fiery temper. But how could I tell you that? I was sure you would run away, laugh in my face. I had to be so very careful not to scare you off.'

The nub of his thumb was wiping her tears away, but it couldn't keep up with her inexhaustible supply. His soft lips were shushing her now, dusting her cheeks like velvet paws, and she ached to press her cheek into his hand, to take the comfort he was imparting, but still she couldn't.

'We understand each other now; that is all that matters.'

'No, Luca.' Her words were strangled in her throat, and he fought to reassure her.

'From this we will learn, move forward together. It might not seem like it now, it might seem scary and overwhelming, but in time you will see it is surely for the best.'

'For the best!' Her eyes opened to a stranger. 'How can you say that it's for the best? How can you just dismiss our baby? But then I guess you've had some practice. Anna told me how you demanded she have an abortion when she thought she was pregnant…'

His face darkened. The hand on her cheek stilled as he let out a low hiss.

'Never!'

'Signora?' A pretty nurse was at the bedside, her eyes smiling, her surprise at Felicity's sudden re-entry to the world evident as she blew up a blood pressure cuff around her arm.

Felicity lay there, feeling the impatience emanating from Luca, the tension in the room as the nurse chatted away, checking her temperature, her pulse, oblivious to Luca's increasingly mounting irritation.

'Never,' he repeated, once they were alone again. 'She could never have been pregnant by me. I took care of that—made sure it would never happen!''

'You weren't so careful with me!' Felicity retorted. 'You didn't stop to think of the consequences when *we* made love.'

'Because making love and having sex are two different things.'

His simple explanation halted her; his summing up of the magic they had once shared took some of the fight out of her response, allowing him a small window to continue.

'Anna has done so much damage, told so many lies. If there is to be any hope for the three of us we must ignore every last vile thing she has said. We must—'

'Two of us,' Felicity choked. Correcting Luca was second nature, but his inadvertent slip seemed rather insensitive, and her tears seemed to be coming back for an encore.

'The three of us.' Luca sat back down, his eyes never leaving her, one strong, warm hand moving so very gently down to her tender bruised stomach below the starched white blanket. Its warmth, its quiet strength didn't cause the pain she'd anticipated. Instead came a sense of security and support, and the muscles that had tensed as he'd moved relaxed under his hand, moulded into the soft comfort of his touch.

'It's too soon, Luca,' Felicity sobbed. 'Too soon to be making promises we can't keep. Too soon to be talking about other babies when all I want is this one.'

'It is all I want too.'

His hand was still on her stomach, gentle, protective and infinitely safe, and as a small smile rose on his face, more breathtaking than the morning sun rising over Moserallo, the bleeping of her heart-rate on the monitor picked up. Somewhere deep inside hope flared, a tiny fluttering, stretching its wings, as Luca softly spoke.

'What do you think is wrong with you, Felice?'

'A miscarriage.' She struggled with the word, struggled with the images so hazy in her mind. 'When I came in the doctor said…' Her mind searched its recesses, dragging the painful memory to the fore. "*Gravidanza ectopica probabile.*" I didn't need a translation dictionary to work out that it was an ectopic pregnancy, that my tube had ruptured. I signed the consent form…'

'*Probabile.*' He was smiling so widely she almost joined him, almost dared to believe that Luca really could do everything—Luca really could put this right. 'It means probably,' he said softly. 'The one little word that is every doctor's escape clause. Only in this case they were only too happy to be proved wrong. You had a ruptured appendix, Felice. Yes you were sick. Yes, we have been worried about you and the baby, of course, but that was all it was. The baby is safe.'

He knew what she'd been through, understood that her doubt in no way reflected on her love for him, understood that the rivers of her pain ran deep, and that sometimes his word simply wouldn't be quite enough.

'Wait there,' he whispered, kissing her softly on the cheek.

'I don't exactly have much choice.'

He was back in a moment, back with the nurse, who smiled kindly and gently lifted her gown, squirting jelly onto her stomach as Luca held her hand.

'Now do you believe me?'

She would have answered, would have said yes, but

tears were streaming unchecked now as one shaking hand touched the screen, trying somehow to capture the future, all her hopes and dreams, right there before her eyes.

'It's so tiny,' Luca said gruffly, and there was a definite catch in his throat as he stared in wonder at the monitor.

'"From little acorns..."' Glancing across the pillow, she stared at his profile, stared at the man who loved her gazing upon the child they would love together.

Come whatever.

EPILOGUE

'Jo's getting very spoilt.'

As they ambled along, their hands entwined, the early-evening sun casting an amber glow around them, catching the sprinklers jetting in to life and watering the lush green golf course, Felicity was grateful to the glare for the excuse to wear her sunglasses and hide the inevitable tears that came each and every time they left Australia. Not that she was complaining—Luca didn't turn a hair whenever a wave of homesickness hit, and the air path between Italy and Australia was a rather frayed carpet.

'I don't think you can spoil a six-month-old.' Felicity smiled. 'Dad's just enjoying having him around.' Luca's hand tightened around hers and she squeezed it back gratefully.

'I wish I wasn't so badly handicapped.' Luca sighed. 'Your dad just laughed at me when I said that, but I'm going to work on it. I'm going to improve my game if it's the last thing I do.'

She didn't even bother to correct him, but a smile chased away her threatening tears at the image of Luca and her father on the golf course. Richard, a true-blue Aussie in every sense of the word, still scratched his head in bemusement at some of Luca's odd ways. Still, *gnocchi* with carbonara sauce Santanno-style was proving a big hit on the menu, and it was nice to see Richard smiling again after so many difficult years—getting to know his son-in-law over a game of golf, and bypassing beer for a glass of good Italian red and chatting long into the night about football and golf and all the things men strangely held so dear.

'You know, after Joseph died I never thought my parents would be happy again—I mean really happy. Content was the best I could hope for. But seeing them with Jo…'

'They're happy,' Luca said softly. 'Of course there will always be sadness there, always be a big piece of their lives missing, but Jo has been a gift in so many more ways than we could ever have imagined.'

He was right, of course. The purgatory of morning sickness had seemingly been left behind with her appendix, and Felicity had enjoyed the final six months of her pregnancy being spoiled, loved and adored by her doting husband. Jo had burst into their lives two weeks late after a trouble-free labour, and had been making up for lost time ever since—smiling at the world, charming everyone who came near with his dribbling smile and mass of dark curls, his dark, dimpled olive skin and eyes that melted even the hardest heart.

'Let's meet the neighbours.'

Felicity frowned as Luca started to walk more purposefully now, turning into the driveway of a massive sprawling property that adjoined the resort. The field was laden with vineyards, the huge rambling home in desperate need of some TLC, but the elderly couple who owned it were too old and too tired to get around to it. She bit back her irritation. This was supposed to be a romantic walk, time to take five before Jo's evening bath and her parents' farewell dinner, not a get-to-know-you session with the neighbours.

'Doesn't seem like anyone's at home.' Luca frowned,

knocking on the massive doors and peering through the dusty window.

'Maybe they're at the resort.' Felicity shrugged. 'A lot of the locals are going there for dinner now that the place has picked up. Oh, look…' A small sigh escaped her lips as she eyed the table on the veranda, the clean white tablecloth and breathtaking flower arrangement out of place amongst the clutter. Two long-stemmed glasses just begged to be filled from the bottle of red wine open beside them. 'I hope we're that romantic when we're in our eighties.'

'We will be,' Luca said assuredly, smiling unseen as she fingered the petals on the flowers.

'Imagine sitting here in fifty years, drinking our own wine, watching our grandchildren and great-grand-children running around.'

'Careful what you wish for…'

Felicity looked up. 'I didn't mean here,' she said quickly. 'I'm happy in Moserallo. I just didn't realise the Murrays had it in them, that's all.'

'Oh, the Murrays are romantic all right,' Luca said, picking up the bottle and pouring two deep glasses. 'They've decided to sell up and move to a resort in Queensland. They want a pool they don't have to worry about cleaning, wine they don't have to worry about bottling, and a house they don't need to think about cleaning. They just want to enjoy each other.'

He looked at her bemused face, handing her a glass. After a moment's hesitation Felicity took it, colour mounting in her cheeks as Luca led her to a chair.

'I'm handing the hotel chain over to my brother.' For an age he didn't elaborate, just stared at the view—the sun bobbing on the horizon, shadows stretching across the vineyard, a cooling welcome breeze soothing the dry hot land. 'I can't do it any more. Can't fire up like I used to, can't leave for work at six and not get home till ten any more, when the only place I want to be is with you and Jo. I know how hard it is for you, leaving your parents, and I know you've never once complained about the hours I put in. But I know it hurts you.'

Finally he dared to look at her, relief flooding his features when he saw that she was smiling. 'We won't starve. I'll still be on the board of directors. But it's too much for one person—things were starting to get missed, look what happened to your father…'

'Luca.' Her soft voice cut into his well-rehearsed speech. 'You don't have to keep apologising for that. It wasn't your fault, and anyway it's over now. My father is happier than I dared imagine he could be. You don't have to justify cutting back to me, and you certainly don't have to give up your career to keep me happy. I'm not so reliant on you I can't amuse myself.'

'I know you're not,' Luca grumbled. 'Sometimes I wish you were.'

'Well, I'm not. I love you, Luca. I love being with you, being married to you, but I'm not going to collapse in a heap if you're not home by five each night.'

'You miss your parents, though?'

'Yes,' Felicity admitted. 'But it's not as if I don't see them.'

'Remember when we got married? Remember sitting on that plane when I said I'd never hurt you?'

Felicity nodded.

'Leaving here hurts you each and every time, and in turn it hurts me. I understand where you're coming from, Felice. There's no shame in wanting your family near—it's what we Italians do best.'

'What about your family, though? If we relocate here, aren't yours going to be just as upset as mine?'

Luca shrugged. 'We'll go home and see my mother all the time. Anyway, there're hundreds of Santannos—countless grandchildren vying for her attention. It's kind of nice here when Jo's the only one. We can make this work, Felice, with my business sense and your accounting skills. Ricardo has taught me a lot about wine over the years. I have discussed it with him and he's happy to offer advice. From what the doctors said at his last check-up,' Luca said with a teasing smile, 'he'll be around to offer advice for the next twenty years or so.'

'Anna's going to have a long wait for that inheritance.' Felicity grinned back, her smile fading as Luca's expression grew more serious.

'I really believe we can make a go of this.'

'So do I,' Felicity murmured, dreams and plans dancing in her mind. She surveyed the familiar land with new eyes now, imagining Jo and his brothers and sisters yet to come running along the veranda, Luca beside her each and every day…

Facing the future together.